*The gatekeeper comes out to you, he grasps your*
*hand,*
*takes you into heaven, to your father Geb.*
*He rejoices at your coming, gives you his hands,*
*kisses you, caresses you,*
*sets you before the spirits,*
*the imperishable stars...*

*The hidden ones worship you,*
*The great ones surround you,*
*The watchers wait on you*

- From the Egyptian Pyramid Texts, Utterance 373
*Lichtheim, Miriam (1975). Ancient Egyptian*
*Literature, vol 1. London, England: University of*
*California Press.*

# Prologue

Tiger and Tarren were tied together by an invisible thread. Their father sat them in the dirt and told them:

"I have linked your fates."

They were starving then, and she remembered those times with the most clarity. Her and her brother had been fighting over a dead sand spider that she had found pressed into the clay. Her father had separated them with his massive hands.

"A person can do one great thing during their lifetime, one magic thing." He had said from sallow cheeks. "That tethering was mine. And now, whatever happens, you must always be together. Together you will be strong and survive. But you must care for each other above all else, or the magic of that thread will falter. The thread must not be broken. Your lives depend on it." Then, her father had eaten the sand spider himself. The words stuck with them. They would never fight over food again.

As she grew, Tiger had doubts about her father's magic. She would go hunting with Sai or her father and feel nothing. If anything, it was good to be away from Tarren sometimes. Tarren and his stories – prophesies about the return of Saxon Arroway or the birth of The Starchild. But then sometimes she would feel it. An invisible force, pulling. She would be checking water collectors or digging for dustcrabs, not far off, the Tar Garden still visible, when suddenly she would feel it – something pulling, maybe pushing her to her brother. Sometimes she would go. Leave her work and find him. He would smile as if to say, *you felt it too?* Other times she ignored the feeling. If she was lucky, it would simply fade away…but occasionally, it became overwhelming and her head would begin to hurt.

She was rarely far from Tarren. Life in Tar Garden became more stable over time. They grew through the years as one starved wanderer after another joined their settlement. Eventually, the settlement grew into a village. Her father became *Ghan* simply by reputation. Nobody worked harder than he did to make shelter, gather food and stave off attacks from raiders. But raids became less frequent as the drought and heat of the Tarlands increased. They would have died or been forced south if not for the well. It had taken months to bring the stone from the ruins of the great northern city. Tiger and Tarren hadn't been permitted to go, but Aichlan told stories of a twisted, frightening place, haunted by ghosts, hybrids and thousands of cats; cats whose bites or scratches could cause death in sunsteps. Of course, he had admitted to only having seen the cats.

When the well was complete, everyone in the village was afraid to drink the water. It was cold and looked clean, but a rumour spread that Tarland water was still poisoned by some black magic from the times of impurity. Some had even refused to help build the well. In the end, it was her father and the old man, Sai, who had sealed the last of the stone and built the frame for the line. That day, her father had lowered, and then hoisted the wooden cups Tarren and Tiger had painstakingly carved from Bittergum tree root.

"It has been hundreds of years since this land

was poisoned and burned." Every face in the village was tired and lined from thirst, but all eyes followed her father. He lifted one of the cups to his face.

"This water runs deep under the earth; it has been protected from the decay of the wastelands to the north. We still need to maintain the collectors, but this is what we will drink now." And he had tipped the cups to his lips and drank noisily in front of them all. The water had splashed down his cheeks, in runnels through the layered dust that clung to his skin. For a moment she had seen Tarren's youth there, in her father's bright fearless eyes. When he had finished, her father breathed a sigh of relief and exaggerated refreshment.

"Don't be afraid. It is cleaner than anything grey that falls from the skies here. Cleaner than any of the meat or roots we can scrounge from the Tarlands. Drink it and be renewed." The people had crowded around.

Time passed in the tar desert. Tiger grew. The village grew. She wondered about the world to the south; drank in the travelling traders' whispers of giants, monuments and people in underground hiding. She thought less of the invisible thread. Sometimes when her father was away on a hunt, she would wander from the village, always farther each time. But the landscape didn't change much. Flat. Empty. Hot. She knew that some day, if she wasn't allowed to see something of the world, no matter how dangerous it was, that she would have to leave. She convinced herself that thread or no thread, eventually that would happen.

Then, two days before Tarren's becoming ceremony she had felt something beckoning her away to the south, like the call of an invisible but conscious force. As she was sneaking off, determined to explore further than she had yet done, her nose started to bleed, and she fell to her knees. All she could think of was her brother. Something seemed to force her back to the village. She staggered into the hut she shared with Tarren and her father.

"Sister. I was just thinking of you."

Tarren was there with the entire village library spread before him: seven discernible books but also scraps and fragments, some of them so swollen and faded they were difficult or impossible to read. That didn't matter much, as Tarren and her father were the only two in Tar Garden that could read a word.

"Tiger you're bleeding."

"It's nothing."

She leaned against the smooth grain of the polished wall. Tarren just looked at her for a moment, and then he crossed the small space in three slow steps.

"I have something for you." He said, holding out his large dark hand.

She reached out, but he pulled back. The late day's sun had shone from the doorway in a wet smear across her knuckles.

"Hold on. The blood. Here."

Slowly and carefully he used part of his tunic to wipe first her hand and then her upper lip.

"It's stopped." He decided, then carefully handed her a small rectangle of yellowed paper.

"What is it?"

"Your words. Your poem. It is called a poem."

"But Tarren, father…"

"Forget father."

He smiled then, small wrinkles at the corners of his eyes. When he smiled, he looked so much like father and so forgetting was difficult.

"But I can't read."

"It doesn't matter. You know the words."

This was true. He had read it to her so many times. *In what distant deeps or skies...*

"Thank you."

"I brushed the page with Sap of Arden, but you should still keep it dry."

"Why are you giving it to me now?"

"Because words have power. They will keep you safe."

Tarren crossed back to the table and began his small ritual of returning the documents and books to their home. He carefully wrapped the treasures in bigleaf. Three layers. Then he reached up to hide them in their place between the roof supports, sat cross-legged on the floor and gazed out the door. They both watched the moving forms of the people as the village began to prepare for night.

*He can't know that I sometimes think of leaving. Can he?*

"Why would I need anything to keep me safe? Is there news? Have raiders been seen?"

"No, nothing new. But change is coming."

"You've been listening to old Miriam again."

"She said Arroway would return. It's been foretold."

"Father doesn't believe much of what she says."

"I know Tiger. But it isn't just old Miriam. It's the air and the deep sky beyond. They tell their own

11

story."

"And what story is that?"

"That Arroway will return. When the Starchild is born, Arroway will return and unify humankind."

"The stars told you all this?"

"And then the Starchild will conquer death. Think! What if the Starchild were born here? In Tar Garden? Who knows, it could be yours! Or mine."

"I'll never have a child, Tarren. But your becoming is at hand – and at least four of the women here would love to try to make you a Starchild."

He blushed at her chiding, still only a boy.

"I believe that there is renewal coming. We can't live in this clay wasteland forever, Tiger. We deserve to be delivered of it. I've seen the shapes of coming change in the sky."

"You are seeing things again. You stare up at the stars too much. You think about *them* too much as well. The best we can do is to hope that soon they will be gone."

"That's what she said. Miriam. That the time of *The Watchers* was at an end."

"Well, then that is one thing I hope she is right about. But can things ever go back to what they were before, like in the stories of old times? When they built a glass tower that touched the sky and the world was filled with food of all colors and magical things." She laughed.

"But then the stars threw down their spears." He said quietly.

"You are too serious. Let's go help prepare for the meal."

She pulled him up and embraced him.

"Thank you for this, Tarren."

She folded the poem carefully into her belt. He smiled, but his eyes were far away.

"Come on." She pulled him out into the late day's heat.

A few days later, Tiger woke early, before Tarren and her father. The night before had been Tarren's *becoming* celebration. The men and women had given him some of the dream fungus, found only at the edge of the Inner Band. The celebrations had gone late into the night. She had gone to sleep earlier than the rest, uncomfortable watching the way the women looked at her brother now that he was permitted. Today, the entire village would sleep like the dead. She lay just before first light, eyes wide open, and heard that silent horn, calling.

She set out to the south to explore. Her father would assume she was west, checking rain collectors. The rains came infrequently but sporadically, and a storm cloud had been spotted the night before. She walked, then ran. Even in the early morning, the sun could be harsh. Today her piebald skin tingled and soon the camp was only a brown bump on the horizon. Around her she saw nothing save the occasional distant rock, treacherous depression or uneven mound. These she avoided. Predators had been known to lie in wait in these places, animal and human.

When she stopped to catch her breath, she scanned the horizon and thought she saw a wild cat moving in the north. But she blinked and there was nothing. Just a sun-wimple, perhaps. To the east, the terrain seemed to change. There were what could be

13

hills. She knew based on the stories of some refugees that had found their camp, that if she went far enough that way, perhaps days, she would see mountains.

She pulled out her poem. Climbed to the top of a large stone. Took a deep breath. She performed the words, just as they were on the paper. But she didn't chant them quietly as she normally did. The paper seemed to give them more power. She shouted them to the empty landscape to the south. She put extra force into the end of each line when there was a similar sound, as Tarren had taught her. When she was finished, nothing happened. The desert of clay still slept. Her face was hot. In her haste she had neglected to bring water, a good sign that today was not the day she was meant to leave. She wasn't even sure that she was meant to leave. The feeling of being called had not faded. It was simply gone. She would have to go back. The sun had already traced five steps across the sky. She could make it back in four sunsteps and in time for the evening meal if she ran hard. Her father was likely to have discovered her absence by then. He would be angry with her. As she stood by the stone, she thought she felt it again, the pull south. Then, a sudden pressure came into her head and she cried out, fell to her knees. This was different. Something new.

"Tarren."

She breathed between stabs of pain. There was trouble. She managed to get up and began to run. She ran without stopping.

She saw the smoke a long time before she could make out the shape of the village. A few spans after

14

she could smell burning flesh. She sobbed as she ran – screamed – but her voice was only the shadow of a dry whisper. Her vision swam as the feet of her leggats smacked the rubble-streaked clay. *Raiders.* They could all be dead. It was her fault. She had left them. Closer now, but still maddeningly far off. She didn't see anyone moving.

Then the wind changed. She saw forms slumped in the clay outside the village. She tried to call out, but the wind swallowed all sound. One of the larger forms broke into two. One half rose from the ground, seemed to regard her, then began running towards her. She didn't even realize that she had taken her bone-knife out. But as she neared the other running form, she saw that it was Sai, the old man.

"Look away child…Look away…"

# PART 1
*"Come and See"*

# Chapter 1

*Tyger! Tyger! burning bright*
*In the forests of the night*
-William Blake

First, they had to bury the dead…thirteen, including her father. The bodies of two dead attackers they pulled outside the bounds of the village and left to rot. By the end, her arms shook and she had nothing left to cry. Sai said some words. She slept, perhaps two sunsteps at the foot of her father's shallow grave in the light of her still burning hut. Her mind, unwilling perhaps to rest despite the punishment done to her body that day, brought her a dream.

*The village burned fiercely, as though anew. In the sky, the moon seemed to expand towards her. She could see them come and go in its glow, The Watchers in their vessels. At the edge of the firelight, shadows moved. She peered into the darkness…tried to call out for Sai…couldn't, as though her skin had grown over her mouth. The shadows moved closer out of the darkness. Four beasts, each different in size and form, crept towards her. She tried to get up and run, but first her hands melted into the clay, then her feet. The first of the four hulked close on twisted limbs, its yellowed eyes locked on hers. Her skin tightened in against her flesh, as though trying to flee from the beast. Its jaw, filled with reddened teeth, twisted open.*

*"Come and see." It said.*

She woke. A shadow moved quickly toward her against the dim glow of the last of the fire. Tiger screamed.

"A dream Tiger-Ghan, only a dream." Sai clasped her by the shoulders.

"A nightmare." She said, looking around at the dark mounds. "We go. Now."

For two days and nights, Tiger and Sai chased the raiders across the clay. The first night was a moon-night and they were able to follow easily. The clay was heavy with the marks of many feet. With thirteen dead, that made twelve prisoners. The next day, they found signs of a brief camp.

"We are almost seven sunsteps behind." Sai said, picking through the remains of the fire with his bone-knife. "They will make the first trees of the Inner Band by nightfall.

"I have never seen a living tree." Tiger said. Though she knew of the different types of wood. Her father had taught her.

"If you truly mean to follow them, we will see little else from the borderlands on. Nothing grows here in the Tarlands – but inside, everything does."

"We don't just follow Sai. We kill. In the dark. They have to sleep sometime."

"There will be many."

"I won't force you to stay with me."

"You won't have to, Tiger-Ghan."

"Don't call me that, Sai. I'm not my father."

"But you are, in your way."

They didn't sleep that night. It was easier to

travel in the dark and out of the heat. The moon was always there, watching them. It didn't move from its position in the sky. The Watchers came and went from somewhere far south: red green streaks on the horizon.

The third day they moved slowly, exhausted, finally lying down to sleep in the shade of an outcropping of rock. Tiger had no dreams. When they woke and pressed on, she noticed that the ground was becoming uneven. Scrags of brush began to appear.

"Sai, I see someone." She stopped him.

"No Tiger. That is a tree." They came closer. The old man was right.

"You have good eyes for an old man."

"Or you have poor eyes for a young girl." They laughed, but the sound was no comfort. She wondered if laughter would always ring hollow now.

Her first tree turned out to be a twisted branch sticking up from the ground, nothing of the green she had been told of. But more trees were to follow. Many, many more.

That night they moved slowly…The Watchers had taken the moon away and the darkness was absolute. They had to stop for a time, or risk losing the trail. Sai was able to make torches, but it took him some time to light them. While he worked, she closed her eyes. There was something new in the air here. It took her some time to realize that it was moisture. It clung to her face and her sides as she lay against a broken, yielding tree. She may have slept. When they had light, they began to move. The trees grew thicker. Tiger heard animals hissing in the dark. An old fear gripped her.

"Sai. Are there lurks here?"

"Not yet Tiger. These are only wild cats. The lurks are further in. They haunt the deeper tangle. They love darkness."

"The cats...will they try for us?"

"Not unless we both go to sleep. They are small, but don't get close. The bite is poison."

"There are so many of them."

"Once they were a friend to man. But when The Watchers first came, there was chaos in the human world. These animals prospered. But their love of dead flesh changed them."

It was at the end of that slow-moving, exhausting night that Tiger spotted, very distantly, the light of a fire.

"Not such bad eyes after all, young Ghan." Sai said, leaning against a sapling that had twisted its way up from inside a much older and very dead tree.

"How far, Sai?"

"Hard to say. Perhaps nine sunsteps from here."

"Nine?"

"Yes. They know these places. They also know that to stay long in one place is foolish. It will be difficult for us to catch them."

"Come on. Faster."

"No Tiger."

Sai put out their torch. The distant fire was now the only thing she could see.

"Why did you do that? We have lost enough time already."

"If we can see their fire Tiger, they may see ours. Better they don't know that any follow them."

It was useless to protest and impossible to keep to the trail in only the starlight. They slept one sunstep each; taking turns keeping the cats at a distance with the many small stones that now littered the ground. Tiger made a game of trying to hit the ones that came too close in the ribs. But the first time she succeeded, one creature directed a surprisingly deep growl in her direction and regarded her with glowing eyes (*come and see...*) – so she stopped.

The next day, the fourth since her father's heart stopped beating, they made better time and passed out of the sparse vegetation and into the true jungle of the Inner Band. After years daydreaming about glimpsing a life other than tar and dust, here she was in the forbidden place. As the bush thickened and the land became rocky, the first thing Tiger noticed was the sounds. Animals. Everywhere. All kinds. And she could see some of them. Birds of many colors when she had only seen black. Things that scurried. Swinging things that laughed. Every sound made her uneasy. With her bone-knife, Tiger made a small cut on her left arm to mark her passage into this place. Then changed her mind and cut three more. One for each day that passed without her brother. Sai only looked on. Nodded.

About midmorning, Sai's foot kicked something loose from the dirt. He bent, scooped it up and held it out for Tiger to see. It was about the length of her arm from fingertips to shoulder. Mostly, it was tarnished and filthy. But when Sai rubbed at it with his tunic, it began to shine. There was a light in his eyes she hadn't seen before.

"This is metal, Tiger. From the old times.

Somehow the sweepers must have missed it."

She had never seen metal and held it briefly with fascination. It was cold and hard.

"What is it for?"

"I don't know." He frowned. "But it will be good for clearing bigleaf when we get into the true jungle. And if we had a really hot fire, we could make a blade of it." His eyes lit with some memory of another life. She hadn't seen him so animated before.

They walked as fast as they could in the now hot, moist air. Sai named the trees and plants for her from the depths of his memory as they grew thicker: Longshoot, Yew, Poplar, Crab-bush, blade-bush, skunkgrass, kill-weed, bigleaf, short beech, cripple-vine, Enoch's poison, splinter-spike and the list went on and on. Most she had never heard of. Some, like short beech and Crab-bush, bore deadly fruit. Some like Cripple-vine and Enoch's poison bore delicious fruit. At Sai's insistence, she tasted some. Her stomach growled for more.

"Funny. The ones that sound the worst are safe?" She reached for more of the tart red fruit.

"Yes, but be careful not to eat too much. It has been a long time since I have been this far in. My memory may be faulty...or the fruit may have changed its mind."

Not far from where they rested, was a small but swift moving channel of water. Sai pointed this out to Tiger. A feeling like wonder filled her heart as she lay on the ground and pressed her hot face into the cool current. She drank deeply. She splashed her chest and arms. She felt revived. It was difficult to leave the small stream. She had never seen one before.

By the time the sun reached its lower steps in the sky, they were both dripping with sweat again. The moon might belong to The Watchers, but the sun was as reliable as ever. In the late afternoon it created strange shades of color that played between the leafy green. Tarren would love the forest...in better circumstances. Tiger held her arm out into the light and the uneven pattern complimented her patchwork skin...

After staring at her arm for a time she realized she had stopped moving. Sai was somewhere behind, tiring. She could hear him calling out faintly between breaths to her. She felt as though she could feel the pull on the imaginary thread that tied her to Tarren. As the sun dipped lower through the trees, she even felt for a moment that she could see it, stretched from her chest out into the tangle, gleaming with tension, ready to snap. The raiders that had taken her brother would know the route through the jungle, as Sai had said. They would move faster now.

Tiger began to run through the sweating big-leaf, her eyes darting from the heaving rooted ground to the tangle of the hillcrest ahead. Pink light stabbed through the gaps in the green and she knew the day was dying fast. Drawing air deep into her chest, she pistoned her legs and fought for the summit. If she could just get a trace of them before the light died, she could determine how far ahead they were. She vibrated with exhaustion.

Behind and below, she heard Sai hacking his way through the foliage with his new prize possession. He was wheezing badly trying to keep pace. Eventually she might have to leave him behind.

She reached the summit, nearly hurtling off the edge of a sheer drop, just able to grab hold a slender longshoot. Pink light stung her eyes and burned her skin. The landscape that rolled away in front of her shone. The trees, moist, reflected the setting sun. She had never seen anything like this in the Tarlands. If the longshoot hadn't been waiting here, she would have tumbled into that lake of leafy glass.

She snapped back to reality. Her father's crusted blood still coated the dirty grey front of her tunic. Her left arm throbbed. As her breathing slowed, she watched the tops of the trees and any clearings for signs of movement. Nothing. All around her the light was being sucked out of the world.

*Where are they?*

The trail led here to this cliff edge. They must have veered left to get down.

*Then where?*

Straight again. Into the cover of the thickest jungle. The light was in its final narrowing now, a rotting purple. Tiger scanned the trees once more even as she heard Sai calling from halfway up the hill.

There. Movement just past center of her field of vision. Slight swaying of the treetops. She marked the place in her memory even as black inked into the purple and the sky died. In the last of the residual light, Sai collapsed heaving in front of her against the same longshoot. Then all went dark.

They climbed. In the dark, Sai was able to find

a good tree, a strong yew with many branches. At his insistence, they climbed higher than Tiger thought necessary. There was one good hollow high up, a welcome surprise.

"You rest here, Tiger-Ghan."

"You don't have to call me that."

But she took it, propped her head and shoulders against the damp inside of the tree. Her lower legs dangled off the thick branch. Sai was likely to stay awake most of the night watching. He sat propped between two forked branches, and though she could barely make out his outline in the cold glint of the starlight, she knew he was admiring the new tool in his scarred hands, turning it over, sliding his palm along its length. She heard it rasp rhythmically against his calluses.

Later, she woke, seized Sai's wrist and guided him firmly into the hollow. He protested thickly through his exhaustion.

"Tiger-Ghan..."

"Silence. Sleep old man, or you'll be no use to me."

She took the stick of metal from his hands. He fell into the hollow, already asleep. She balanced in the crook of the tree and listened. The jungle below was alive with sound. That was a good sign. Sai had told her that when lurks were near, the jungle went silent. They were high enough in the tree that any beasts (*come and see*) would have trouble reaching them. Yet her fears – based only on the memories of stories of running from the lurks, told by the others around the fire – remained. In the dark, her mind called forth its own images. *Teeth on bone. Bright jets of blood.*

She strained to hear the sounds of people: talking or perhaps low laughter. But they were not foolish enough to make a fire so deep inside the green, so she didn't expect them to be reckless enough to attract attention with loud sound either.

Tiger had always preferred the moonless nights...unsettled by the hive-like activity and fiery green streaks of moon-nights. She had always found it hard to sleep when she could see it; wondering what The Watchers were doing there...what new horrors they may choose to unleash. She hoped that the raiders would also be forced to rest at night and that Tarren would be smart enough not to fight them.

There was a snap from below. Something large and heavy was moving up the hill near their tree. She stopped breathing. In the hollow, Sai was rasping thinly, almost inaudibly. She wanted to reach out and wake him but couldn't risk it. She gripped the thin rusted metal, Sai's treasure. But it wouldn't make much of a weapon. Below, there was more crackling. A heavy movement. A grunt. Was something climbing the tree? *Come and see.*

Out in the darkness, a high-pitched scream sounded, and was then cut short. The sound cooled her already chill bones. She tried to make note of the direction. Could it be from the same place she had seen the swaying treetops at lights-end? At the sound of the scream the yeeking and tittering animals of the jungle went silent.

Below, there was another grunt, almost like words, and then an explosion of energy along the ground as something large moved quickly through the trees in the pitch-dark. She heard it moving down the steep slope, breathing heavily. After some time, the jungle returned to normal and Tiger heard nothing but Sai's ragged breath.

By daybreak, Sai was awake and imploring her forgiveness for sleeping, particularly in the hollow.

"Tiger-Ghan, it is unacceptable. Your father-"

"Don't talk about my father right now, Sai. I need your help. You can track. But if you can't keep up with me, I'll leave you behind."

"You must not do that. You don't know all the dangers of the Inner Band."

"All the more reason for you to keep the pace old man." She began to climb down into the steep ravine and after a moment, Sai grunted and began to follow.

# Chapter 2

It was mid-morning of the 6th day. Another cut. She made it deeper. But Tiger felt the press of time more intensely, fraying against her father's thread, like an enormous bone-knife held by a giant hand in the sky, stretched down sawing. She knew that her brother would never become like them, would never forgive. When they reached their lair, they would try and fail to break him to their purpose – and so he would die.

They were inside the Inner Band now, where life was controlled by The Watchers. There were snaken everywhere, of every color. As promised, Tiger could already see more varieties of tree than she could have ever imagined. Sai, of course, knew them all. This raggedweed has poison nettles. This gumtree delicious purple fruit – but only on the branches near the top. Tiger listened to him struggling to explain and move quickly at the same time.

"Sai, stop. Tell me when we rest."

"I thought we were resting." He said, and wiped his sweating face with the back of his hand.

Faster then. But navigating the steep slope was difficult. Tiger picked her way carefully, moving laterally away from Sai as she descended. If he slipped and fell, the two of them would careen to the bottom in a mess of shattered limbs, lucky only should they break their necks. Tiger reached the bottom and crouched in the soft green moss. Below her leg, something moved. She remained still.

"Tiger Ghan, the trail is still fresh, I can see-"

"Don't move Sai."

He stopped. Looked down at his own legs in the moss to mid calf, saw the rippling. Tiger heard the soft slake of dry skin. The moss bed stretched forward into the bigleaf. Everywhere there were what Sai had called Tepi trees, draped with looping vines. The mossbed writhed, a gently moving mass of greens. There was no wind this morning. Sai was still as stone; sweat beaded his brow. Tiger's thick leather leggats would provide some protection. But Sai was barefoot.

"I'll come to you. Don't move."

She stepped lightly, testing inside the gyrating mass. Now she could see them, sliding in and out, over and under. One step brought a quick hiss and commotion of blind strikes under the moss. She could see that Sai was trembling slightly, though his face appeared calm.

"Perhaps we should run." He said quietly.

Tiger's silence was refusal. Two steps closer, eight more to go. She nosed the toe of her leggat into a mass of them, prodded for ground, found only more movement underneath. Finally, she reached the old man.

"Climb onto my back Sai."

"Tiger-"

"Now."

He obeyed. She felt his leathery skin. His wrinkled dry arms scraped the smooth hard round of her shoulders. He wrapped his legs around her and hooked his ankles. He was light. The ease with

28

which she bore his weight frightened her. She leaned forward, bracing him…stepped more cautiously than before, looking for the shortest path out of the nest.

"There." Sai whispered, pointing to a mound of rocks off to the right.

Tiger began to move slowly towards the rocks. She mistook one hard and still form for ground. There was a chorus of hisses and a Diamondhead reared up, struck. There was pressure on her calf. She stopped. Waited for release. The leggat was layered for harvesting in the northern snakenpits. She was unharmed. This time. But many of the snaken here were larger than in the Tarlands. She saw one half as thick as herself move through a thin place in the moss. The sun shined on a lidless emerald eye. Closer to the rocks now. A cloud of flies appeared as they neared the rocks.

"Those are not rocks." Sai observed. Tiger pressed forward through the moss. A leg appeared, a seat, part of a shoulder. She stepped up onto the dead man. The flesh was swollen, a deep purple hidden under dusty grey cloth and green moss. She paused on the man's back. Long stealthy forms slithered out of the green, over the body and back in again.

"It isn't Tarren."

"No Tiger-Ghan. It is Daniel. Was." A wave of revulsion washed over her, and she hurried off the corpse.

Thirty more tense steps and a few strikes later, Sai slipped down and off from her back. He quickly moved to remove her leggats.

"No Sai, we must continue." She pushed his

hands away. "I am fine."

"You would not feel the poison. We must be sure."

He grabbed at her foot again. Tiger kicked him away, lightly.

"I said no."

"Ok, ok."

He put up his hands, grinning with a gapped mouth. He stood and surveyed the tangle of bush.

"The trail. You said it was fresh."

"Very. I could see well the path they traveled as we came down the cliff."

Crouching, Sai moved quickly through the undergrowth, the calluses of his bare feet rasping against the ground.

"Here." He was gesturing to some split grass bushes. "They passed through here."

"You're certain?"

"Yes. Very. Look here." Sai pointed to the tangled ground. "And here."

Tiger saw nothing there but nodded.

"Your legs are bare; you won't last long in the deep bush." She said.

"I will be fine."

"Oh? Without me just now, you would be next to Daniel."

Sai didn't speak, just continued to examine the split grass. Tiger moved back into the moss. Soon she was back at the body. She performed a quick and careful search, found nothing useful. Then, forcefully, she guided the leggats off the dead man. His legs were bloated from the poison. Sai crouched patiently, watched.

"Put these on."

Sai complied. They were loose on his frail legs. Tiger's bone-knife gleamed white in the morning sun. She cut a length of vine, then crudely laced the top of the leggats. Daniel would have approved.

"Thank you."

"I can't read nature like you can. All I see is green and mud. Don't die please."

The jungle steamed as the sun rose. They waded through bigleaf and something Sai called natfern that released clouds of bothersome stinging bugs into the air in front of them. Tiger's stomach growled for food, still they pressed on. Sai moved quickly but they could not run, the bush became so thick. Here, the trail became more obvious to Tiger as the brush thickened. She saw broken branches, trampled bigleaf and the occasional break or scuff to one of the long twisted roots that crossed their path everywhere. After a long time they came to a clearing. Embers of a morning cook fire. Sai crouched by the fire, poked the embers with his metal treasure.

"How long?" She demanded.

"Six sunsteps. Maybe less. Less."

"If we catch them today, I will kill their Ghan."

"Tiger, we must be cautious. They are too many to rush upon. Darkness will be our friend."

"My father's death must be answered."

"It will be."

"Without a leader, they will scatter."

"Maybe. But there is risk to Tarren."

Tiger moved closer to the fire. She crouched down with Sai, tried to see what he saw in the dirt and the ash.

"Teach me this."

So he showed her the depressions, the particles, the layers. After some time they knew what was eaten: a large cat.

"But not a wasteland cat. A jungle cat, nearly your namesake." Sai grinned.

She pressed her hand to her waist to check for the words. The poem was still safe there. It was the only physical connection she had left to her brother. Perhaps the thread was wrapped around it, unspooling as her brother was dragged further south. *Twist the sinews of thy heart*...

They knew how many were in the group, twenty-two, maybe twenty-three, plus the now eight bound captives. That meant they may have missed several bodies somewhere in the jungle. Or perhaps not. Maybe the large thing she had heard moving in the bushes in the night had...that Tarren could be one of those already dead was not a possibility she was willing to consider.

There had been ill treatment. Sai showed her the place on the ground where there was sex. Another place in the dirt where there was a fight or torture.

"They will use our women hard. Perhaps the men as well. Your brother and Aichlan likely protested the treatment and were beaten, here." Sai moved his hand in a circle above the ground.

His face was sad but calm, as though he had seen all of this before, in some past life. Tiger felt anger growing in her chest. Then she pictured her father...dead...and tamed her anger. Saved it. She would need it.

Midday. They moved on, the sun tingling their skin through the gaps in the trees. The bush thinned and they were able to run again. Sai with his steel toy moved in front now, whacked aside the grabbing green fronds. Tiger tried to be patient, but soon was out in front again. She felt the slow haze of the steadily progressing afternoon with a panic that defied the movement of time. She felt she must reach her brother by nightfall no matter the sunsteps that remained between her and him. Sai called directions ahead to her, sometimes forced her to stop. She was dodging the increasing pools of swampy and foul water when she heard a curse from behind. She stopped, dragged in a breath and turned back.

"We need to stop, move back. You are going too fast again." Sai said.

"Keep your eyes on the trail." She spat back.

Sai moved back into the leaf, muttering under his breath. After some time, he found the trail again. They stopped briefly to eat. Sai found many wild plants and some delicious fruits, many of which she had never seen before. She asked him why the traders never brought them such things.

"The fruit traders that visited us would never come this far in." Sai said, through a mouthful of sticky purple fruit. There was plenty. It was more than Tiger had been accustomed to eating. There were stones, smooth and flat for them to sit on. They sat side-by-side, facing south. In the depth of the jungle, something screeched.

"There is so much to eat here, Sai."

"Yes."

"Could we not have lived inside? Could we not have survived here?"

"No."

33

"Why would we live so far out in those filthy, barren plains, struggling every day for meat, when there is so much here?"

"You know why Tiger."

"You sound like my father. We must beware the lurks. Beware of gangs and raiders."

"Yes, them too. All of them. This place, these things -- The Watchers did not make them for us."

"Perhaps the old woman Miriam was telling the truth. She said they would be gone from the world soon. But I have never seen a lurk. And as for safety from the gangs…"

"A raid was always a risk, one your father knew well."

"Not well enough then. Look where it brought us."

She spit the hard seeds of the dark triangular fruit at the flat of the rock. They bounced like pebbles into the greenery.

"This jungle is a deadly place. *Their place*. And we are not yet fully inside."

"You survived here, long ago. When it was worse. My father told me about you."

"I was alone. And survival can be a very near thing." Sai gestured to the wide twisted scar across his midsection.

Tiger had seen it before, run her hands over it as a child.

"What did they try to take out of you, Sai?"

He didn't answer. They finished eating. They shared from her leather water skin.

"Tell me about Saxon Arroway."

"Hmm. A legend. Built up in people's minds."

"Was he a real person? Tarren believes he

was."

"Perhaps. Probably. But not this prophesy nonsense. He's not going to come back from the dead and lead us all to salvation."

"No," she said, pulled the old man up by the arm. "Let's keep moving"

The light was beginning to fade again and after a time the trail became difficult for Sai to find in the swampy ground. Tiger's hope that they would catch the raiders before sunfall was fading. Her panic came and went in a useless cycle. Their leggats were caked with mud, their feet inside swollen and sweaty from abuse.

"How close do you think we are to them?"

"We are a few sunsteps from them yet."

"Can we not push on?"

"Impossible. The sun will fade. We must be in the trees by then."

"There are some longshoots ahead, taller than these *yews*."

"Safer, yes we can stop there."

Tiger entered the grove first. Here, there was almost no underbrush. The ground was covered with wide puddles, reflecting the pink of the tired sun. She had never seen so much water in one place in her life. At first, she thought she was looking at hummocks scattered across the dim glade; twisted mounds of root and earth heaved up by the soft ground.

"Sai…"

The words died in her throat as she saw one of the hummocks shift. What looked like an arm came free from the ground. Had they stumbled upon the gang sleeping? Could Sai have been so wrong in reading the trail?

Ten spans in front of her, another mound moved. In the dim light, she could barely make out the form and certainly no features. But she saw the clumps of earth fall from the shoulders and heard a guttural growl. More forms began to shift up from the earth, some dripping with the stagnant water. Then she saw the dim blue glow at the neck through the mud, the red shine of the eyes. Lurks. A nest of them.

She turned; Sai was frozen behind her. Seeing with her. They locked eyes.

"Just run." He whispered. "To the west. Don't stop. Lose them and head south again. I will find you."

"Sai–"

"Run Tiger. And if you can, climb!"

There was another growl and then suddenly the shapes in the dim were shooting forward. Sai sprinted off to the east. Still frozen, she watched as some of the dark forms tracked left with incredible speed after Sai. Some were still moving toward her. Her legs felt joined to the ground; her shins melted to the mud. One of the things uttered a sharp, loud barking sound. The sound unlocked Tiger's legs and she sprinted west, towards the thicker jungle. The lurks followed closely behind. She ran blind into the dark jungle. Cuts and slaps of the foliage. Ragged breath. Panic. She was losing the trail by the moment, and felt her brother moving further away from her. Felt the slack in the thread drawing up.

Choking on her own sweat, Tiger fell over a patch of bramble high enough to gouge her thighs. Panic seized her body, but somehow, she found she could pull herself underneath the thick twists of bush. She was panting, waiting for the lurks to find her and tear into her head with their razor claws and dripping snouts. She unsheathed her bone-knife. Held the ragged but hard blade against the thrumming artery in her neck. She wouldn't let them eat into her face while she lived. One quick snick across the neck. It would be fast. She wondered if Tarren would feel the thread break. If he would carry it and spool it up the rest of his life.

Time passed. She heard cracks, distant. Grunts. Far off barking growls. Then, nothing. She had lost them. Her breath came more evenly, through dry, cracked lips. A green glow began to grow in the sky. She had no way to mark time. It was a moon-night, but The Watchers guided its movement by some pattern unknown to her. The full round orb glowed green in her view. Faint streaks passed to and from the horizon as she could make out through the distant tree line. Red trails dissipated and fizzled to black only to reignite on the horizon as fiery lines that she could see even through the thick tops of the trees. There was no accompanying sound. Her head began to pound as she watched them come and go and she shut her eyes against the sear of the green. She slept.

They were around her when she woke. She could hear them moving through the bramble to her left. Shaking trees to her right. There were many of them. She wondered if Sai had made it to safety, perhaps high in the branches of a tree. They came closer still. Could they smell her blood? She pressed mud against the cuts. Her bone-knife found her throat again, waited there. Cold. Time passed, and the lurks did too, deeper into the bush. She waited. Re-sheathed her bone-knife. Crawled out from the murk under the thorns. She moved through the jungle, the dim green shine let her see a few feet in front of her and no further.

She was lost. Stumbled forward dumbly, fighting back tears. A tree loomed in front of her. She wiped her eyes with the back of her hand. Two red orbs gleamed at her from the tree. A mud-rotten smell filled her nostrils. Her hand went to the knife at her thigh. Frighteningly strong arms seized her, and a conical mouth appeared in the green haze of the moon. The face was horrible. She saw the faint blue pulse at the back of the neck, the swollen translucent sac. She knew exactly how she was going to die. Saw the formerly human teeth, elongated, all sharp. They would drive into the center of her face; tear in through her eyes and her nose. What was once a tongue would then stab out, pierce deep into the frontal lobe of her brain, slither along the base of her skull and take its prize. And that's when the thread would snap too. She was sure Tarren would feel it. Her eyes closed. She tried to repress her own desire for final resistance. She felt its hot and sickeningly pleasant breath. Like ripe fruit.

Then there was a sound. A twang. A wet thud. The grip loosened. Tiger opened her eyes. The shaft of an arrow protruded from the eye socket of the lurk. It grunted, the jaws yawned wide, the tongue lashed out towards her face. It fell into the mud, pulling her down. She strained away from it, slapped its powerful claws from her skin. Too late – the weight of the lurk brought her hard toward the ground. There was a brief sharp pain as her head struck something. The glow of the moon. Blackness.

# Chapter 3

*In what distant deeps or skies*
*Burnt the fire of thine eyes?*
-William Blake

She woke. He sat in front of her. In the dark, her vision blurry, he was only a pale shape in purple shadow. She reached to her thigh, but the knife was not there. Whoever sat in front of her had saved her life. And whoever sat there had also taken her knife. It wasn't Sai. Tiger tensed herself to spring forward. So much time had already been lost. The trail was growing cold by the sunstep, the jungle filling itself back in over the passage of the raiders. If Sai was not dead, and even if she could find him, they may never find Tarren's trail again. Soon the thread would break forever.

To overpower the form in front of her, she would need simply to be fast and to be ruthless. She was in some kind of a sheltered crescent of rock and bigleaf. There was no trace of the lurk anywhere near them. This person sitting in front of her had carried her through the dark. A man then? Man or woman, both were likely to use her ill. If she was fast enough, perhaps she could simply disarm him. She stole herself to do anything necessary to win the struggle. Positioned her foot. Her muscles tensed.

The form in front of her spoke suddenly. She couldn't understand the words. They sounded so much like Anglese, and yet as though they were spoken from a snake-throat. She opened her mouth and closed it again. Breathed once. The voice repeated the same words and this time, though the words were drawn out and had a hissing quality to them, she could make them out.

"Don't be afraid," said the voice. "Don't be attacking us."

The form shifted slightly, and Tiger caught a glimpse of a large yellowish eye in what little moonlight pierced this thick part of the jungle.

"Who are you?"

"I am called Gralen."

Tiger suddenly realized that she was not speaking to a man. Or a woman. The thing in front of her on the rock was a hybrid. Both human and watcher. An abomination whispered about and feared.

"Yes. Gralen, both it is."

The thing spoke as though not used to the practice. Then suddenly, she felt a strange violation she hadn't felt before. As though there was an unwelcome hand on the front of her mind, pressing. Could this hybrid read her thoughts?

"Yes. Speaking not Need. Can not you hear us?"

And then Tiger felt something in her head, a pressure deep inside, between her nose and eyes. A trickle from her left nostril ran easily to her lip. Somewhere she registered its metallic flavour. Shapes like words formed in her head. Her vision swam and something pulsed behind her eye.

"Stop that...it hurts." Immediately the pressure stopped.

"Gralen take your knife. Give it back."

The thing on the rock shifted and Tiger tensed. An arm came forward in the dark; the light from the moon caught the white gleam of her knife. A thin

41

grey hand held it out, in offering.

Tiger took the blade and some of the tension left her body. The hybrid did something with its face that could be a smile; in the dark all Tiger was sure of was a glimmer of teeth.

"Thanks many."

She didn't sheath the knife though, but kept it ready. There was a void of silence now. The hybrid remained still in front of her. She felt the push against her mind again.

"I said not to-"

But then a message came through clearly. Then another. An entire conversation seemed to attach itself to her mind. Her spine stiffened of its own accord and she felt the trickle renewed in her left nostril. She opened her mouth to speak again. Then realized she might not need to. Some time passed that way, with her head locked to its head. She couldn't say how much time, only that the night slowly vanished.

The sun had yet to break through the dense canopy overhead, but Tiger and her new companion were already moving through the cool shadows. It was always coolest just before dawn, and silent; even the snaken were still at this time. Tiger could still see almost nothing, now that the moon had left the sky, but Gralen led her. *Gralen*. That's what he called himself. Claimed he wanted to help her. *Don't trust him*, warned her other voice. Though without Sai, she needed him.

Soon light licked through the canopy and caressed her face. Though in only sunsteps she would long again for the cool of the dim morning, now she welcomed the sun, the only lover of her

42

piebald skin. Later, the heat would sting the freshest of the seven cuts on her arm. But Gralen shied from the light even now. He moved in the parts of the tangle that retained the night's darkness; canopied yew trees with walls of stab-leaf and stagger-vine. They traveled through twisted ravines of moss growth. Here and there was an old road pierced in hundreds of places by diamond-root. Something inside her head was sore. It was a good kind of pain, like the pain that came after running, or after a hard day's labour.

She thought of digging up clay-yams for her father, and the physical ache in her head was dwarfed for a time by something larger. She couldn't help but think of her father's body; all that remained of him now was a decaying mound wrapped in animal skins in a shallow grave. She told herself he lived on in Tarren. The son was the spitting image of the father. Tarren would look just like her father when he became a man. His voice would deepen and one day boom when he laughed, the lines around his eyes would sink into the skin when he became serious, just like her father. Their father. That is, if those that had hold of Tarren hadn't already...she couldn't think like that. She would think of something else. But what?

Sai. He could be alive. And he was, aside from Tarren, the last living reminder of her father. Always at her father's side, Sai was subservient in a sullen but diligent way. Her father had saved Sai from one of the techno tribes, from the lost sons of Arroway. Two men had been trying to take something out of his body. Her father had interrupted while he was hunting. The men, hands

43

slick with Sai's blood, had been no match for her father, who had moved through the jungle on silent, practiced legs.

There had been a long recovery. Sai a ghost under uneven sheets of dried leaf, cold clay packed over his wound. Tarren had been young and so forbidden to see the warped scars twisted across Sai's stomach that leaked green pus. But Tiger had been often in attendance under that canopy and saw the old man sweat and writhe in fever. Watched her father, sometimes others, carefully wash the angry scars with the bitter water of red-fern oak bark and then repack the wound with fresh clay. Eventually, she had learned to take care of him. Had washed the green wound and packed red clay on it and dabbed cold mud on Sai's forehead.

A cold grey hand clamped onto Tiger's forearm and she jerked back to the present. Gralen stood in front of her, closer than ever before. In the light she could see its seemingly poreless skin stretched tight across an oblong face. Its head stretched unnaturally far back from its smooth brow. It smiled and for the briefest moment the expression was so like Tarren's...then the sharp teeth caught the light. They were stained – likely from the same juicy purple fruit Sai had shown her grew in abundance here – yet the color was so like blood. Tarren vanished then. But for a moment, she had seen something human. The hairs everywhere on her skin moved. She took a step back.

"You frightened me."

She was thinking it too, opening her mind to him temporarily. It was easier than before. He was hot, needed to keep cool, find a place to rest. The

44

area ahead was dense with snaken, they must move around it. What was worse, there were great ones ahead.

"Great ones?" She asked aloud.

It was only the closest translation her mind could make of his thought, which seemed like a hundred meanings compressed into one. They had stopped on a small rocky hill. The trees were thinner here, the scrub brush thin. Gralen leaned back against a tall, cool rock, out of the reach of the sun. Words pressed into her head.

*Those that work and build.*

*Is there a danger?*

*Always danger in the world.*

*From The Great Ones?*

*Yes.*

Tiger realized Gralen meant the giants. Her father had called them Lurk Kings. Sai called them Nephilim.

*Yes. Giants. Many ahead. Not safe for Gralen, or for human.*

*How do you know they are there?*

"Gralen sensing them from far. They haven powerful mind."

The hybrid's speech was clearer than before.

"How close are they?"

"See..."

"I don't understand."

"See! Come"

*Come and See.*

Gralen pointed ahead through the trees, towards the high end of a ravine.

"We can see them from there?"

"Come."

They moved upwards and Tiger saw that Gralen was right; there were more snaken here. One stabbed out with its fangs at her ankle; she mashed its head with her heel. Another dropped on her from a tree, its fangs latching to the leather strap across her chest. With a quick motion – to hesitate meant to die – she twisted its neck and removed the head with her knife as she walked. She knew this snaken, covered with red spots and highly poisonous. There were a good many in the clay pits to the north of their village. Good eating, if one was sure to remove the poison sacs. She could use the poison if they found the gang. She wrapped the head in a large yew leaf, then slipped it into her small leather pouch, beside the poem. None of the snaken attacked or came near to Gralen.

They came to the top of the ravine. Gralen raised a thinly muscled arm into the bright sun and pointed to the valley below. Then it retreated to the shade and squatted down on the ground, watched her with its large yellowish-black eyes.

Tiger stepped out into the sun; a wave of heat seared the sweat to her already hot skin. At first it seemed that the treetops in the distance were moving, but there was no wind. Her eyes were bleary in the blinding light. She pressed the backs of her hands to her damp eye sockets. Then her eyes adjusted and she realized that she was not seeing trees.

"So it is true."

Her bone-knife fell from her hand and stuck into the leaf littered ground. Her mouth remained open. She slowly regained her breath. They had come to a place where the jungle was thinner and down from where she stood, further than she could throw a stone and yet somehow too close, the giants were moving.

"I thought that the stories were only meant to scare us. To keep the younger ones from following into the jungle during the hunt."

Though she wasn't exactly speaking to Gralen, the hybrid stirred and came nearer to the light.

"Great Ones serves us."

"I don't understand."

"Great Ones is us." Gralen smiled through eyes misted from the stinging light.

"Us? You mean like you? Like me?"

Though she didn't speak it aloud, she felt another moment's revulsion at the thought that she and Gralen were alike. She wondered if he knew what she was thinking. She was getting better at feeling when it was in her head. She couldn't feel it then.

"Yes. Like us."

"And they serve people? So will they serve me?"

She looked down at them again, there must have been a hundred or more of them, moving through the trees, pushing them aside like long grass. They seemed to be carrying something.

"No. Serves us."

"Serves you? You and me?"

From this distance she couldn't quite make out their faces, but the giants looked human enough to her. They were all naked except for a loin covering of some kind. They all seemed to be male.

"No. See."

There was pressure on her mind again. She

opened her mind, understood. The Watchers had created the giants. The giants were their workforces. The giants were their slaves.

"They work for them?" Tiger pointed up to the skies.

Gralen nodded.

"And you are one of them." Tiger said.

Gralen's teeth came together, and its lips twisted into a half smile.

*Part them. Part you. I am lost.*

*These giants were once people like me?*

*Yes.*

*I don't understand, how have they been changed?*

Gralen closed its eyes, brought its fingertips to its temples and Tiger's mind flooded with information. She fell to the ground, her left knee smacked against a mossy rock and her jaw hinged open. The breath was forced from her lungs. She saw it all simultaneously (*come and see*) and felt an immense pressure in her skull...couldn't make sense of... felt her left eye bulge...blood explode from her nose. Her vision swam. Falling. Gralen moving quickly toward her, like a massive snaken.

# Chapter 4

*On what wings dare he aspire?*
*What the hand dare seize the fire?*
-William Blake

The sun was high in the sky when Tiger woke from unconsciousness. Gralen was kneeling over her and she felt its cold touch on her skin. Panic seized her but before she could respond to its chill flesh, it drew away from her. The panic faded. She glared at it distrustfully. Her head felt like a crushed orango, the only sweet fruit that her father had ever been able to bring back from traderuns and her favourite. She had loved being asked to step on them at mealtimes; she would crack the hard shells and scrape the fruit into the communal bowl. Tarren used to wash with the peelings and he had always smelled of the crisp fruit. She could smell it now. Her head throbbed. It was the seventh day.

"What did you do to me?"

Now she felt information crowding her mind, sudden unwanted but remembered knowledge, as though from a recent nightmare. It all hit her at once and violently forced the memory of her brother to evaporate. She leaned over, retching.

"The lurks...the giants...people, we are all the same – stages in their service. Your brothers. The Watchers. The Grey Devils."

She spat this last, staggered over to the large tree she had held before, tried to catch her breath. Gralen didn't speak, only regarded her cautiously.

"Only – your kind...they are different. And so you...you are different somehow too. From some

49

other place. Far beyond here. Far, far away."

Gralen nodded and moved closer to her. He reached out a thin arm and beckoned to her to step closer to him. Tiger was not sure why she thought of Gralen as male. Its lack of distinguishable breasts was the only physical indication. A loose-fitting leather wrap was all the creature wore to hide its genitals, if it had any.

"What? What do you want now?"

But she moved closer anyway, despite her instinct to refuse.

"No more now...I don't think I can handle any more."

Gralen nodded and was reaching out slowly, carefully, for her head. The grey hands seized her again, but this time the pain in her mind disappeared immediately. She could think clearly again. The pulsing, blinding ache that had sat behind her eyes was gone. The thin arms drew away again.

"Better."

Gralen watched, curiously, as she cut another thin line into her arm. *Seven*. Then they both returned to watch the giants trudge along. The day was hot, and they had not found the trail. Now the path ahead was blocked by a long, seemingly endless line of walking monsters.

"The lurks collect something from us...in our heads. When they get enough of it, they take it...somewhere...south. Then these giants are made."

That wasn't precisely it. Gralen nodded though, close enough.

"I want to get closer. I want to see them up close."

"This bad. We stay away."

"We will be careful not to be seen."

Gralen shrugged, but she could feel its desire to travel by another route. They began to descend into the ravine. The trees were thinning here on the side of the hill. At the bottom the trees became sparse in a way she hadn't noticed since the borderlands between Tar Garden and the Inner Band. As they moved closer, she was able to better distinguish the giants from one another. Each of the hulking forms wore some kind of loincloth made from a material she didn't recognize. The material gleamed, seemed to absorb and hold the light.

The air was filled with grunts and a low rumble. It took Tiger a moment to realize that they were talking. Some of them were laughing. She could not understand their language. They spoke it mostly with their lips curled back or mouths open, their dialogue a hundred gentle collisions of harsh sounds. It was almost as mesmerizing as the shimmering cloth. Gralen hunkered low at her side. Tiger could feel its fear, greater now than before. After moving closer, she looked back and realized that Gralen would go no further. Tiger proceeded on her own, crouching low to avoid being seen, moving silently in her leggats through the denser places in the underbrush. The trees were much thinner now and if she were to stand up, she would risk being seen.

The giants walked like men. But their bodies rippled with muscle in ways she had never seen. The arm of one of the giants was larger than Tiger herself. She thought of how easily one of them could crush the life from her body. Yet still, she moved forward, filled with curiosity. The giants were still laughing, marching with huge burdens of stone. Each of the blocks they carried was larger than she was. Some of the Giants, in groups of three or four, carried even larger blocks. These giants were sweating and grunting and moving more slowly than the others. Then, incredibly, a giant stone appeared at the edge of her vision. It looked to be larger than her father's hut had been back in their camp, perhaps twice the size. But she saw no giants. This stone was floating through the air. Surely Gralen had damaged her mind – this could not be possible.

She raised her head above the bush. The last stone was indeed the largest of all. But Tiger was wrong that there was no giant moving it. The giant seemed to be the last in the long parade. He held something long and slender, like in length to the browned steel Sai had found. She couldn't be sure it was metal, as it was shining with golden light. The end was rounded and the giant had it pressed against the stone. She heard a low humming. As the giant passed her, the small hairs on her arms and the hair tied behind her head seemed to vibrate towards the stone, the golden rod or perhaps both. The sound seemed to vibrate in her bones, and she couldn't help letting out a gasp. The giant turned and Tiger dropped back into the green.

"Abur-Mahkt. Hekt-do!" The giant bellowed out. Tiger's first thought was to run. But she knew she couldn't outrun this creature, not with the trees thin like they were here. She needed the deeper tangle, something that would slow the large things down. So she pressed even flatter to the ground instead. She looked for Gralen and saw nothing. She should have listened to its warning. From where she lay, she could see the legs of the giant. Then another pair of legs appeared, running back towards the first. She tensed, clenching her bone-knife. Tiger could not see the stone, but she knew it was there. She could still feel the hum, everywhere in her body. The two begin to speak in abrupt, harsh sounding tones.

Then the second giant suddenly ran off ahead once again. Tiger's grip relaxed slightly. The first giant yawned. He hadn't moved. Suddenly she saw the stone come lower into view. Then lower. Finally it seemed to be resting on the ground. The hum stopped and a massive thud rippled across the ground. Tiger shook with it. And then, the giant sat down, back against the stone. She could not see its face, but heard it let out a long, exhausted breath.

*Maybe it didn't hear me.* Tiger waited. Aside from the giants deep and slow breathing, there was only silence. Perhaps the giant was sleeping. If she didn't go now, she may miss her only chance to escape alive. With the practiced silence her father had taught her, she came to her feet in a crouch and looked over at where the giant was resting.

But the dark-haired giant was staring right at her. His eyes settled directly upon Tiger's. She was too frightened to move or even to breathe. Something deeply intelligent within his gaze made Tiger shudder. The eyes were old; as if there was knowledge there that Tiger could only dream of. In that one instant she was filled with the surety that the giant knew more about the world than she ever would.

The corners of the Giant's mouth turned up in a half smile. His eyes did not change however, and remained locked on hers. Tiger waited, her pulse pounding. The sweat on her skin multiplied. She heard the lack of sounds around her in sharp focus. Her muscles twitched, and despite her fear, she was ready to run if she must. She hoped that her body would listen to her mind.

The giant said something. His words were unintelligible to Tiger. He did not move from where he sat. He glanced around, peering into the edge of the woods and the tangled underbrush, looking to see if there were any others. Then, the giant spread his massive hands—palms up—and raised his eyebrows. The sound of the other giants moving had faded into the forest ahead. Somehow, Tiger found words.

"Hello." She said quietly. "I am alone. Do you speak my language? Can you understand me?"

The giant smiled wider.

"Ah. It has been a very long time, but I can speak in the older English."

"I'm sorry to disturb you. You won't hurt me?"

"Hurt you? Oh no. Of course not. Unless you can see a reason that I should do so."

"You are a giant. You could crush me if you wanted to."

"Giant."

"What do you call yourself?"

"You may call me *Nahim*. This is close enough."

"Nahim. Do you mind my asking where are they going? Why have they left you behind?"

"On the contrary, why have I ordered them

forward?" He narrowed his eyes and looked at her expectantly.

"You are their leader?"

"No. Well, yes. There are considerations. There is the code. The word. The law." He tapped the golden rod that lay at his side.

"You are human. I have not talked to one in many years. I have never seen a human like you before. Your skin is very different. From where did you come? You don't look as the grave-lings."

"Grave-lings?"

"Those that dwell under. I thought maybe your skin is a result of living deep."

"My skin has always been like this. Have you seen them recently? Gravelings?"

"No. I have seen very few of you. The ones I have seen are always running from us Giants, burrowing in their secret tunnels. Gravelings and Cavelings. But you are different. You are pleasant. And polite. I like politeness."

"You are not the ones destroying us? Sending my kind under the ground?"

"We are builders, not breakers. We destroy nothing. We collect, we build, and we work."

"Your masters are the destroyers then."

"All serve *Those Who Watch*."

"I am searching for my brother. You're certain you have not seen a group of humans traveling? I had the trail and have lost it."

Suddenly the giant stood. At his full height, Tiger had to crane her neck up to look at him. She felt her pulse pound. The giant gazed down at her. If she could convince this giant to travel with her and with Gralen, they might find her brother all the faster. The giant would be able to see over many of the trees. Not the tallest longshoots of course, but certainly the smaller fronds, stagger-pricks, bushes and bigleaf.

The giant's face darkened, and he tilted his head.

"Who are you travelling with?"

Nahim took a few steps towards the tangle that Tiger had emerged from. Tiger's pulse pounded as the giant neared her. Every step he took vibrated the ground under her feet.

"What makes you think I am travelling with anyone?"

Tiger looked for signs of the hybrid. It seemed that Gralen didn't want to be seen.

Nahim turned suddenly, an angry look clouding his large features.

"If you want the continued generosity of Nahim, human, then you will cease your lies. I can smell the hybrid. Have it come out."

Tiger could feel a throbbing in her temple. How was this possible? She felt a sudden press against her mind. She let Gralen speak to her.

*RUN.*

The force of the word almost knocked her over.

*RUN NOW RUN.*

Her eyes slammed closed in pain and she pressed her hand to the front of her head. She was dizzy…

Before Tiger knew what is happening, enormous hands seized her and lifted her up off the ground. She felt how easily Nahim could crush her.

"Come out hybrid! I will squeeze the life from this human if you do not."

56

"Let me go."

She struggled to retrieve her knife, but the press of the giant's callused hand pinched her hand and arm against her thigh. Then the giant began speaking in the thick language she did not understand.

"Mallahk-Tesht. Trablick-Wickt, trablick-tallat. Forshtune. Wicktet-Mahkt. MAHKT!

Tiger tried to relax her body and speak to Gralen, to tell it to run. But she had trouble directing her thoughts without knowing where Gralen was. She looked to the bush where she last saw it, thought she saw movement there.

Nahim continued to say the strange word again and again; mahkt, mahkt, mahkt. If this was to be the end of her short life, then she would not die screaming. She relaxed her body and closed her eyes. Tried to picture Tarren. Where he might be. Thought about that thread, imagined herself gathering it in her hands, pulling.

"MAHKT!" The giant shouted again.

Pounding...shaking. A rustle in the bush. Opened her eyes.

# Chapter 5

*And what shoulder, & what art*
*Could twist the sinews of thy heart?*
-William Blake

Gralen stood writhing in visible agony in the sunlight.

"Pakhasht! Gralen. Chik-mo Spekhetha?"

The giant set Tiger down suddenly. As soon as his hands left her body, she was drawing her knife and rolling away from the giant. Gralen shielded its eyes from the sting of the sun. Tiger could see its pale skin beginning to burn immediately in the heat.

"Get away from us!" She yelled, pointing the small bone-knife at the giant.

Nahim regarded them for a moment and then threw his head back in laughter. His laugh was a deep boom.

"Spekhetha Gralen! Imkesh Khetap Eagrr-ma chik-mo gru-tep!" Nahim roared, then threw his head back in deeper laughter.

Tiger looked from one to the other, confused.

"Yes, Nahim. I can speak in human tongue."

Gralen seemed ashamed, continued looking at the twisted earth. Nahim only roared louder.

"Ah, you see girl! I know this hybrid that leads you. A snaken of a creature, shunned by your own kind and also by Those That Watch."

"I don't understand."

"Of course not. This creature has told you nothing of the world. It is likely that it would have taken you deep into the woods, hypnotized you and fed on your blood."

58

"No. He saved me."

But Tiger felt more and more frightened. The world of the Inner Bands was beyond anything she had imagined. Her brother seemed farther from her reach than ever before. Each moment was another of her brother's now limited heartbeats.

"Ahhh, Gralen, for all your newfound powers of speech, you have told this human little of your history."

"How do you know each other?" Tiger gestured to them each in turn with the blade.

Gralen met her eyes with its own yellow orbs. The pupils were slits and the grey skin flamed with red. She felt the pressure on her mind again suddenly.

*Do not tell Nahim you can Hearen Gralen thoughts.*

Tiger met the eyes of the hybrid. Gralen stared levelly back.

"Ah...a blade. Where did you find such a thing?"

Nahim was transfixed by the knife, began to move towards her. Tiger backed away, held it in front of her.

"Don't come any closer, or I will use it."

Nahim's eyes widened and then he broke into more laughter.

"Very well human girl. Please, don't hurt me!" Nahim raised his hands in mock obedience. "How have you managed to avoid her wrath, Gralen?"

"Don't mock me."

Tiger felt heat rise into her face. The giant sat back down, this time on the broken trunk of one of the great trees. It creaked under his weight.

"Apologies, odd spotted human child." Nahim held his hands in a pacifying gesture. "Let Gralen use his newfound ability with the human tongue to tell you how we know each other."

Tiger looked to Gralen. The creature was shaking now, its entire body beginning to turn pink.

"Gralen...get out of the sun." Tiger moved to the creature and helped it to the shade of a twisted tree.

Nahim watched bemused as Tiger helped Gralen sit atop a rock. She removed the bow from its back and shoulder and found a pool of shaded water. Using a handful of sponge-moss, she brought it the cool water. Gralen nodded gratefully and used the moss to cool its skin.

"He can't be in the sun."

"Ah, yes." A small smile played at Nahim's lips and he began to walk. His thick black hair hung down against his shoulders and he turned his face back to them. "Come."

"Where are we going?"

"Out of the sun. We can talk while we travel."

"Then you will come with us?"

"I will guide you some way, but not far. I have stone to move."

"I thought we were as flies to you."

Tiger hesitated at the edge of a tall row of shaded yews.

"You are different than most humans. I find you interesting. The code forbids me to harm this creature." Nahim gestured at Gralen. "For you, my word will have to suffice. Come."

That was enough for Tiger. It would have to be. She helped Gralen and they followed Nahim past the enormous stone and back into the jungle beyond. She was glad to be moving again. Somewhere in the distance, there was a long, drawn out and ominous sound, as though some long lost instrument – like she'd seen in one of Tarren's books – had been raised to otherworldly lips.

# PART II
"The Revelation"

# Chapter 6

*And when thy heart began to beat,*
*What dread hand? & what dread feet?*
-William Blake

The odd party moved for three sunsteps through dense jungle. Nahim at times left a swatch of destruction larger than the trail of the gang they had been following. Tiger began to worry that she had lost the trail when she had lost Sai. But Gralen was confident that he would soon find the trace.

*All must travel the Three Bridges Road for a time. It is the only path South. We must leave. Nahim is dangerous.*

Tiger knew nothing of this road. But she did know that at the moment to suddenly leave the company of the giant seemed far more dangerous to her. So she ignored Gralen for the time being.

"You know Gralen."

Tiger increased her pace and fell in beside the giant.

"Yes, I know him. I am walking you to the road used by the humans; they call it the *Three Bridges Road*. We Eloh-hakim call it the Channel of Death. My people fear that place, almost above all others. I should not like to enter there. But it is your best chance to find those you seek. There should be just enough time for this tale. And I do love stories."

The jungle – which had all but emptied of the

62

sounds of life as the giant made his passage – cloaked them from the burning touch of the high sun. The giant began to speak. As he did, his hands came up and formed exaggerated shapes and movements in the air.

"After the times of the darkness, when the struggle of your people was all but ended, there were those of your kind that persisted, in the dark places under the dirt and rock. In those days, *Those That Watch* came more frequently upon Gaik-tat Mulak."

"Gaik-Tat Mulak?"

"This place." Nahim gestured with his arms to everything around them.

"The Earthen?"

"Yes! Earth, as your ancestors of old would call it. We, the giants – or the Nephilim as you call us – refer to ourselves as the Eloh-hakim. When *Those That Watch* came down upon the earth to awaken us, they were often in the land. At this time the servants, the Hakim, were less in the land."

"What are Hakim?"

"Your people have different words for them. The collectors. The children."

"Lurks? The dog-faced eaters?"

"Ah. Such nasty words for our saviours. Our children. But yes. The humans call them lurks in the Outlands. You must be from there, a child of the scattered. The collectors, or lurks if you must, had reduced you humans to near extinction. *Those That Watch* came down to awaken us Eloh-hakim. But there was one day when something incredible happened." Here Nahim paused and looked to Gralen. The hybrid regarded the giant suspiciously.

63

It had lost its pink sun-angered color and was regaining its former ashen hue.

"The Great War?" Tiger said.

Her favourite of the old tales. For Tarren it was a singular obsession. Around the night fire, Sai had always told the story best.

Nahim narrowed his own eyes at Gralen.

"Be careful of this hybrid. It can read your thoughts. Have you felt pain in your head, here?" Nahim gestured to the front right of his own massive skull. Tiger shook her head, looking over at Gralen suspiciously for effect. She felt the grip on her mind relax and suddenly realized she could trust neither of these strange creatures. *Remember that they know each other.* She told herself.

"The Great War... many events have that title, but only one that would live as such in the recent memory of your people. Perhaps we speak of the same one."

Nahim looked back at them both with eyes that seemed they could measure the depth of time itself.

"The humans came from under the earth in large numbers. They were half-starved and filled with bloodlust, but they were also organized. Under one leadership."

"Saxon Arroway. May he rise once again," Tiger said, unconsciously touching her forehead and thinking of her brother.

The giant stops to consider her.

"Hmm."

From where he was slinking along behind them, Gralen hissed. The snaken-like response was a surprise to Tiger. She shied away from him, watched him more carefully.

64

"Gralen and his kind are few and have reason to hate this name. Saxon Arroway, the great leader of the men from the earth. Yes. I had only just been awakened, a few turns before the attack. I was stretching into my new skin. You can't know what it feels like to be asleep for as long as I was."

"Saxon Arroway was the last great hero. Unless you believe the Starchild prophesy."

Nahim just smiled.

"If you will understand more about the one you travel with, you should hear the story from another side."

"I am listening."

"When the humans appeared from beneath the earth, it was a surprise to Those That Watch. Perhaps they did not watch closely enough. There is a place far from here, a sacred place that you will likely never see, Aluk-Makhit. It is the place where my people are reborn. Those That Watch created this place. Your ancestors tried to destroy the temple. Many of the Eloh-Hakim perished defending it. Many of my brothers."

"My father told me Saxon Arroway broke the neck of a giant with his bare hands."

Nahim threw his head back and a landslide of laughter tumbled out towards Tiger.

"Perhaps girl, perhaps. Yes, stories of heroes and their deeds are often exaggerated. But this human man Saxon is much respected by the Eloh-Hakim for his bravery. He led his men to their death trying to reach the temple of Aluk-Makhit. Many of my kind were killed in the battle at the great river. Perhaps you have heard of it?"

"Yes. That is where Saxon made his last stand.

65

The river Arroway, my father called it. I thought it was just a legend."

"Ah. Not so. I was there, at the battle. To our people the river is The *Elin*. It is our sacred place to bathe."

"You were there? Impossible. That would be almost one hundred years ago."

"I helped build that temple with these hands."

Nahim stopped and regarded his callused and scarred hands, which had been moving in time with his story.

"These temples. Why do you build them?"

"In time…in time. I hope you live to see an Eloh-Hakim temple. It is a wonder to behold. Our temples will exist here long after all of us are gone from this place. The river temple is the gateway to the Aluk-Makhit, and that is our sacred place. There I fought the humans. I took many lives. One brave human gave me this" Nahim lifted his arm and showed Tiger a twisted scar along his side. "I spiked his head at the temple steps in his honour."

"Some say that Saxon survived the Great War and lives still." This was always Tarren's favourite part of the story.

"I have heard many stories. Our legend is that he was bitten by one of the Elin snaken and turned to stone. My people say he still stands defiant in some lost part of the jungle."

They had approached a deep valley that stretched nearly a thousand-span across. Here the jungle thinned. Across the valley, Tiger could see a twisted and crumbling protrusion of stone. It sneered out from the place where the green suddenly grew thick once more.

66

"What is that place?" She pointed.

"The beginning of the *Three Bridges Road*. Where we must part ways. Come."

They started down the slope, Tiger close behind Nahim and Gralen slightly back and to the side, picking his way carefully through what shadow he could find.

"We were winning. The war drawing to a close. But the humans were able to take prisoners of some of *Those That Watch*. We tried to follow into the jungle and killed many of them, but the remaining humans escaped under the ground. We could not follow."

She suddenly realized Nahim had just spoken her greatest fear aloud. If the raiders were to reach the underground network before...

Gralen spoke up then.

"Humans creating us from pain. Tortures deep in the ground."

Tiger regarded his strange features once again – the almost dual nature of his skin tone, so unlike her own patched skin – it was as though Gralen's skin changed with the light. Sometimes the skin looked human. At other times – such as when he had been inflamed by the sun – his skin seemed to...swim...somehow. To shimmer. And in the strange eyes, sometimes she could recognize something: a flash of mutual understanding, or – perhaps – a flicker of suspicion.

"Combine themselves with our destroyers? Why do such a thing?"

"Those Who Watch are – different. They live far longer than you humans. And they live very well without much light."

"Why the torture?"

"Ah. Those That Watch do not reproduce as humans do."

"I don't understand. How do they survive?"

"They eliminated the need to mate long, long ago. They have also taken that from us, for now. But when the building is done, then we go to the travelling place. That is where all is permitted."

They neared the yawning mouth of the dark road. She knew that Tarren had already crossed over that murky threshold. How much time could be left.

"We need to hurry." She said.

They matched her pace.

"So Gralen is what exactly?" Her eyes flicked to his, but the creature only looked at the ground.

"Gralen is one of the few who survived the human meddling, deep underground. Humans should not meddle with flesh they do not understand. Gralen is both human and Those Who Watch. But an abomination to them." Here Nahim gestured upward.

Gralen seemed to ignore them, staring forward, squinting in the light. Tiger regarded its strange features once more: the almost non-existent nose, absence of cheekbones and wide smooth forehead. She imagined she could see more humanity than not flickering there in the bright yellow at the center of the eyes.

"When did you meet him before?" She asked Nahim.

"Gralen once helped to show my people the entrance to the place where the humans created him when we feared they might come again in great numbers. But now humans living under the ground

68

are cut off from one another, Those That Watch made sure of it. And time has grown short in this place."

"Gralen, is this true?"

The creature stopped, eyed them both.

"Truth. Gralen living no place. No place to belong. People wants to kill it. Watchers in sky would destroy it also."

They started moving again.

"The humans under the earth didn't realize how effective their experiments would actually be." Nahim said, starting up the slope towards the road. "They must have been puzzled when they realized that the children born of the human mothers could not mate, just like Those That Watch."

As Nahim spoke, Tiger tried not to glance at Gralen's loin covering and failed. The creature ignored her glance.

"The hybrids became like the Watchers. They favoured the dark. They could move in it quickly and quietly. They could even see in the pitch black of the deepest of the hidden human tunnels. Then came the physical changes. Then the mind control." Here Nahim turned his own gaze upon Gralen. "But I am sure Gralen would not try its tricks on you."

"Why would the humans want to breed themselves with the grey devils?" Tiger said. Nahim paused for a time, looking from her to Gralen.

"You despise them, but they bring life to dark places. They created us, the Eloh-Hakim. They are the gods of this place, your Earthen. They have long been masters of the stars. The people living deep in the ground tried to blend themselves with the star masters because they are adapted to dark places.

And because they knew then what was coming."

Tiger was about to ask what was coming, but Nahim halted them and pointed ahead to two pillars of stone twisted over by the largest and most hideous trees she had yet seen.

"That is where the *Three Bridges Road* begins. It is a long road and some places will be impassable or too dangerous. There you will need to route through the jungle. Gralen will guide you. But you must not trust it."

"Can you not help us?"

"Impossible. Only a fool would go deep into the ruins of that place. The humans hate us Eloh-Hakim. And they are starving. My flesh could feed a band of them for months. I should not expect to see the travelling place if I were to go in. And my soul partner Ashiv is to meet me there."

She looked at him.

"You also have someone you are trying to reunite with. Then you understand why I need to save my brother. I will protect you. Gralen and I both. We will leave this place by the same way we enter it. All of us. There is a kindness in you, I see it. Please, help me."

Nahim looked from her to Gralen, then back at the road again. His hand fell to the golden wand, still sheathed at his waist. And then the familiar laugh came, but it seemed forced, without its earlier trace of mirth.

"I like you. I shall help you on only one condition –"

Tiger simply waited. But before Nahim could name it, Gralen's thoughts were hissing violently in her head.

*NO. You must not!*

The pleading went on in her head, but she pushed it to the back of her mind, stared only at Nahim, calmly.

"Well?" She said.

"When we have reunited you with your brother, I want you both to accompany me to Aluk-Mahkit. To the great temple."

She doesn't ask why. Nods assent. The entrance is both maw of sound and yawn of silence.

# Chapter 7

*What the hammer? what the chain?*
*In what furnace was thy brain?*
-William Blake

*In the dream he was being eaten alive by animals. They had yellow eyes and crawled all over his skin. He sat propped in a tree and he could not move because the animals had somehow fixed him there. They crawled under his skin. They were inside his muscles. They were eating him from the inside out. They were gorging on his special heart. They drank the blue light there, but the heart kept him alive yet. They crawled down his throat, down to his bones and into his spine. They scurried in his guts. Up above, in the dark sky, the moon was hanging. And he could see them, The Watchers, moving over the surface of the moon. As he watched the pain inside of him became intense as the moon moved closer. The trees melted away and dripped to the earth, leaving nothing behind. All that was left of the entire landscape of the earth was the tree that he was stuck to.*

*The earth below his feet turned from a steaming, sweltering jungle to a dry barren wasteland. Not like the occasionally damp clay of the Tarlands, but a dry, lifeless dust. The earth split and cracked. Everything once alive melted and dripped and leaked into the cracks. There was nothing left. Finally the animals inside of him ate their way through his skin and he saw them: their yellow eyes, their small hairless bodies. He realized that they were not animals but people. They crawled all over his body, picking clean all the muscle and tendon on the flesh. They ate in great grabbing handfuls all the tissue they could find. They swallowed the skin until he was nothing but bone and blue heart-light protruding out from the tree. Somehow, he was still able to see, think and hear. He tried to scream but he had no lungs to drive the air. Above in the sky the moon loomed closer and closer. The wind blasted across the deserted landscape, whipping up a cloud of dust. The dust hit him and all of the little beings were knocked off his bones. They flew off and shattered against the dry ground and fell into the yawning cracks. He watched as the bones of his toes and his feet, his legs and his knees, his pelvis and eventually all the rest of him blew away in that relentless wind. All that was left was his heart-cell and his head, somehow fixed atop the rotten dry tree.*

*Still the moon drew closer and closer, and a great roaring filled his ears though they too had been swallowed. He could still hear the roaring getting louder and louder and louder. The moon careened towards him. In the final instant before it crashed into the dry tree, he could see The Watchers, looking down – or perhaps up – at him. Could see them inside their ships and from underneath the surface of the moon. They seemed to smile and laugh at him.*

*"Come closer. Come and see." They said at once in his head. And then he was always rushing towards oblivion.*

Sai woke in a feverish sweat. He was lying on a bed of cold rock. It was the middle of the daytime and the flesh on his arms and his back was torn. He could barely remember, but sometime in the night running from the lurks, he had fallen down a steep cliff. He knew that at some point he had hit his head. Perhaps this was the only thing that had kept him alive. Certainly if he had been conscious all the way down, he would have tensed his body, tried to break his fall and injured himself far worse. He turned and his head was filled with a searing, unbearable pain. He looked up. The edge of the cliff seemed spans from where he was lying. He wondered that the lurks that were chasing him at the time did not make their way down here to where he lay. Then he thought of Tiger and was filled with panic. Perhaps they were drawn to different prey and followed her deep into the jungle? He had not known many cases of men escaping from lurks when in the dark of the jungle. After all, the lurks had the ability to see in the dark. And they were merciless hunters.

Sai tried to sit up. The pain again wracked his body, but he was able to focus his mind through it by breathing deeply. It wasn't the first time that his body had been cut up or bashed around like this. If anything, the fresh cuts in his skin reminded him that he was alive. He stood, a bit shaky. He was a very old man.

Tiger-Ghan. He must find her. He owed what was left of his wretched life to the children of Avo. Avo may not have been a great warrior Ghan, like those that fought in The Great War, but Tiger's father had been a great man while he had lived. He had kept his clan safe – and fed – above ground, something no leader had done for a very long time.

He felt the weakness in his old body starting to

take hold. His blood was thin, and his peculiar heart very tired. The only way to keep it working was to keep it working. He must move. Too much being still was beginning to feel like death. He took a moment to collect his sense of direction. From this wet pit, it was hard to see the sun clearly. Its rays knifed through the split leaves of the big trees and stabbed at the cuts on his arms and sides. If he did manage to get into the full sun, his flesh would burn. He stooped and collected handfuls of cold mud, smeared it on his bleeding skin. At first there was a sting, replaced quickly by a pleasant numbness.

Sai moved towards a gap in the trees. One of his legs dragged in protest, but he ignored it and found he could still run, though perhaps not as fast as before. He would have to move quickly though. If Tiger still lived, she was young and strong and would keep her promise of leaving his old bones behind. Her love for her brother Tarren was perhaps fiercer than her love for her father, though she would have scarcely been willing to admit to that. Sai knew that time was short for the captured. He knew well what the captors had in mind for most of their prizes.

He inclined out of the pit of the valley into a bright flash of light and shielded his eyes. Some of the cuts he missed stung in the sun. After a moment his eyes adjusted and by the position of the sun, he quickly found the southern path. He began to run as fast as his body could handle. He wasn't sure when the power-cell deep at his core would fade and die, but when it did, his one hundred and thirty-year-old body would follow closely behind. Surely there was still time for redemption.

# Chapter 8

*What the anvil? what dread grasp*
*Dare its deadly terrors clasp?*
-William Blake

The road into the jungle followed one of the broken and twisted remnants of the old roads of man. Some old poison lingered there that kept the jungle from growing entirely over its crumbled surface.

"Mustn't eat anything growing near this road." Gralen said, when Tiger reached for some tempting berries.

"Listen to Gralen now. These are his old haunts."

Nahim had grown oddly silent when they entered the thick canopy of jungle. His eyebrows were furrowed and he would occasionally chew at his lower lip with his enormous, square white teeth. No birds or cries greeted them as they traveled. To Tiger, the place had the feel of evil.

"You should trust to Gralen for the tracking, for it knows this land better than I. And still trades with some of the humans, I see." Nahim gestured to the bow Gralen wore slung over one narrow and pale, but tightly muscled shoulder.

"Gralen, do you know which group has taken my brother."

"Tells us of them."

"They raided us in the middle of the day, a surprise attack. We were celebrating my brother's becoming the night before. Some of our men forced him to eat from the poison mushroom that grows

77

under the sponge moss at the edge of the jungle."

"Yes…seeing things."

"It makes you see things, yes. When they came into our camp, many of the strongest of us would have been unable to fight them."

"How did you escape?" Nahim interrupted.

"I was away from the camp. Just wandering. My friend, Sai…my father sent him off to look for me…if I hadn't…maybe I could have…" She didn't know how that sentence could possibly end.

"What's them looking as?" Gralen said.

"I didn't see, but somehow Sai did. He said they all had their hair cut short and had strange round scars on the right sides of their heads."

Gralen made a low sound and moved closer to the edge of the shadows.

"These be the mens descended from those that kept Gralen. I know these ones."

"Can you find them?"

"They liven not far from here. South. Taking prisoners bad. They wanting to kill all hybrids. Hole to the head is to stop the thinking…"

Nahim turned to Tiger as Gralen finished speaking.

"Gralen speaks of the humans that live under what was once a great city before the darkness. They use the old tunnels. This is the largest group of them. They fear the hybrids most of all, for they are descendants of those that created them."

"Yes…but us broken. Lost." Every second word from Gralen's mouth was a hiss.

"How many of you are there?"

"Few left, thinken maybe five."

"I have met only three of them. Gralen, one

called Runor and also one who calls himself The Eaten."

"The Eaten?"

"Yes. He eats human flesh. Has acquired quite the taste for it. His revenge follows the cycle of his hunger. An unpleasant creature all around, you should be glad you ran into this hybrid and not the other. Though if I trusted him fully to guide you safely, I would not have come with you as far as I have."

Nahim met Gralen's eyes.

*He lies.* Came the sudden thought from Gralen.

But the hybrid just continued to look at Nahim.

"Yes…Eaten…bad. Dangerous for all. Gralen also."

They carefully moved on. Every few spans, Gralen would examine the ground. Around them began to appear the ruins of what looked like ancient buildings. Furry animals darted here and there beneath the low bush. The occasional snaken followed stealthily after.

"These gravelings, they have only your brother?" Nahim questioned.

"There are others…members of my clan. The last of them."

"They may already be dead. Or if not, these humans will perform their ritual on those they have taken."

"Ritual?"

"Yes. Every person's skull is opened if they live to adulthood. They stab out a part of the brain to eliminate the ability of the hybrids or of Those That Watch to control the mind."

"I see." Tiger focused on the trees and the long-tunnelled path ahead. *Can't think about Tarren's head being on the receiving end of such a ritual. Must not think of dark skin bright white bone and the berry red blood that would merge the two.*

"The power to control thought is strong. The hybrids have exacted revenge on humans this way before. If the clan travelling make it safely back to their hidden city, which is doubtful, then they will open your brother's head. Sooner or later, if he lives through the procedure, he will become one of them. The life underground is not much known to us, but there is fierce loyalty amongst the clans that live there."

"Nahim, this underground city must not be far. My brother is everything to me, the last of my family. Please, help me stop them from taking him."

A tear spilled from her cheek.

Nahim sighed, regarded her and the hybrid. Gralen was bent to the trail ahead, pretending not to notice.

"I will try to help you, Tiger. But the places under the earth are inaccessible to my kind. If I am to help you reclaim your brother, we must catch them before they reach it."

"How far is it from here?"

"Less than two days march for my kind. But it will be longer for you and your short legs. And should we fail, you must still keep your promise to accompany me to Aluk-Mahkit."

They pressed on. The jungle around became tinged in blackness. As the heat of the sun began to fade and the night gathered in, Nahim seemed to tire. From in the darkness, came animal sounds Tiger hadn't heard before. One was like the happy scream of a child and guttural yell of pain, all at once.

"What's out there?"

"What isn't? This jungle is meant to be a brutal place. You fragile humans should expect to survive no longer than the next sunstep."

"Where I come from is barren, but there were no lurks in the North. My father said we could build a life there. He was right, before he was wrong."

"The Hakim thrive in darkness. They cannot bear the light, long exposure ruins them."

"Yes. And so finally, we found a safe place deep inside of nowhere. A place we thought could be safe."

"And your father became a great leader?"

"The Ghan of our clan, yes. He always denied he was leader, but he saved us all. Found a way to grow food under the barren clay. Made a hole deep in the earth and found water. He kept us strong when hope of survival seemed faint."

"Ah. Yes, a great man. I admire stories of such…people."

"He had to do something. My mother was carrying Tarren then, far too soon. I was still hanging at her chest. A baby."

"Do you remember?"

"Remember what, being a baby?"

"Yes."

"No…I'm not sure when I first remember. I think it might be the night my brother was born. I thought my mother was dying."

"Human birth is a difficult thing?"

"She bled to death during the night, after Tarren was born."

"So much death in the world. How beautiful."

Nahim paused, turned and stooped low, looking right down into her eyes.

"I remember the moment of my birth." He said.

Tiger looked at his moonish features, the stretch of his lined skin.

"I can't imagine the mother that could bear such a thing."

Nahim threw his head back and laughed his chalky rumble.

"Nor is it necessary for you to. We giants are born at The Great Temple of Aluk-Mahkit. We are drawn from the great essence by the power of Those Who Watch."

"I don't understand."

"You have much to learn. I will tell you some things, but the knowledge that hides inside would require…some time." Nahim pointed to his head.

Gralen stood away from them, watching, alert.

"I knew a man almost as old as you. I always enjoyed his stories. But I lost him in the jungle."

"Yes. But perhaps I was not clear before…I was not speaking of the moment of one of my rebirths. I was speaking of being able to recall the time I was first born."

Along the broken road the sounds of animal life had returned, despite the disturbance Nahim created as he moved. But gone were the pleasant sounds of any birds or even the squeaks of the furry things that moved in the underbrush. Now there were croaks, howls and hisses. Every now and then, a tittering laughter echoed from ahead. Tiger constantly thought she could see dim shapes, moving. Then nothing. They came across water –

streams, pools and even small marshes that stretched off into the darkness of the deep forest. Tiger drank gratefully from a thin stream that ran down from a rocky slope a distance from the road. The water was clean and refreshing. She had never seen so much water in her life. As the sun began to set, Gralen began to show more strength, pressing on ahead into the deep bush, moving silently, searching for signs of trails or tracks.

They moved swiftly now. The Moon rose and Nahim had finally settled into a pace Tiger could easily maintain. He was moving at a swift walk, being careful not to let any small trees swing back and hit her. Occasionally a large snaken would strike out from the rubble and the green at their feet. Most of them tried to sink their teeth into Nahim's ankles or feet and found themselves frustrated by thick, weathered skin. Tiger's boots served their purpose and she was able to collect a few more snakeheads. She would draw out the poison from the glands in the heads when they stopped for the night.

Pressure on her brain. Gralen back in her head, shouting.

*STOP.*

She froze and dropped low, behind a slanted stone. Nahim was still moving. Gralen hissed at him and waved a thin grey arm. After a slight delay, Nahim stopped and sank to the ground. Now they were all silent, listening.

Tiger flexed her mind and thought to Gralen.

*What do you see?*

*There is humans.*

*Can you see them clearly? Is it them? Do they*

*have captives?*

*Maybe being. Maybe not so.*

*How many?*

*Wait and stay.*

Gralen moved away into the bush, its bow ready at its side. Nahim and Tiger waited. After some time, all they could hear was the mocking titters and unpleasant buzz of the jungle. Tiger moved up beside Nahim.

"He has been gone awhile." She whispered.

"You cannot trust this hybrid, Tiger."

"He saved my life."

"Always the hybrids are concerned with survival. It will open your neck with its teeth in the night if it thinks there is some benefit."

"And how do I know you will not do the same?"

"You don't. But I will not. I am enjoying your company too much. I enjoy good conversation." The eyes of the giant did not seem to lie.

From ahead in the jungle they heard a short cry. Tiger started to rise.

"Wait."

The giant held her back gently with a rough hand. After a moment, Gralen appeared as if from nowhere.

"Comen now. These done. You see."

Tiger and Nahim followed. In a shaded glade, two bodies lay in the fern. A third, a man, was pinned to a sickly tree by one of Gralen's slender arrows. This man's head was drooped. As Tiger came closer, she saw the heads of the men on the ground; they were a mess of blood and bone. She turned, not having expected the sight. Took a breath and looked again.

"Gralen...what did you do? I thought you were just going to follow them and watch."

She strode towards him angrily and he hissed, backing away.

*They was bad humans.*

"I don't care! If they are part of the group that took my brother, they might know something important!"

Tiger realized that she had responded aloud to Gralen. Too late. Nahim's eyes narrowed.

"Don't let this hybrid speak in your head Tiger! It could destroy your mind."

Nahim moved towards Gralen.

"Speak your thoughts aloud Gralen, or I will destroy you in spite of *The Code*. Stay out of her head."

Gralen backed away with narrowed eyes. When it reached the man against the tree, it grabbed him by the hair and raised the head. The man's eyes began to blink and Tiger realized he was still alive.

"I saving this one for you to ask!"

Gralen dropped the man's head and he groaned again. Tiger stepped closer, looked at the man's head carefully.

"He is not one of the tribes that took Tarren. He doesn't have the mark."

Indeed the man's head was clean.

"The hybrid did this, look." Nahim held up the shattered head of one of the fallen men.

"I know, Nahim."

"No, the hybrid did this...with its thoughts."

Tiger looked to Gralen, realized it was true. Looked to the dead men. Their skulls looked as though they had exploded from the inside.

The man against the tree was fully awake now. He looked from Tiger to Nahim to Gralen, and then began to scream. Gralen quickly clamped a pale hand over the man's mouth. Tiger leapt forward.

"Listen to me! Be quiet."

After a moment the man stopped. But his eyes remained transfixed on Nahim and the hybrid.

"If you scream again, then this hybrid will do the same to your head." Tiger pointed down to the arrow sticking from the man's abdomen. "If you want to live, you will do exactly as I say."

The man nodded. She looked to Gralen and it removed its hand from the man's mouth. The man spit immediately and then retched.

"Please...I'm opened badly...water."

Tiger carried a crude waterskin, but it was empty because this part of the jungle was filled with water. She pulled it off and threw it to the giant.

"Get him some water."

Nahim looked at her, amused, then bowed his head and moved back through the trees.

"Gralen, search them." She pointed to the bodies on the ground. Gralen was less enthusiastic about obeying Tiger, but after brief hesitation, did what she wished.

She turned back to the man on the tree. He was losing color quickly. If she removed Gralen's arrow, the man would not last long.

"Who were you travelling with?"

"Please...water."

Tiger reached out and gripped the sides of his face with her hands, forced the man to meet her eyes.

"Speak or there will be none."

"Just my clan. My brothers."

"Your clan, do you raid others?"

"What?"

"Do you raid? Do you steal from others?"

"Lurks…always above…in the night…the Eloh-Hakim passing. In…day. Eat. Water. There are beasts…we are starving –"

"Do you take people? Do you steal them?"

"No. Only food…"

"Have you seen a boy? A younger boy, almost my age?"

"…only food."

"Where were you heading?"

"Home…we went to raid an eastern clan…but they were dead. Starved. There was nothing."

Tiger looked over at Gralen; he was busy searching the bodies.

"What kind of child…travels…with a hybrid and…the Nephilim…?"

"Have you noticed a gang passing through here? A large one?"

"…heads…yes…"

The man trailed off, his eyes rolled up. Nahim returned with a skin full of water. Tiger grabbed it and threw some water in the man's face. He returned to consciousness with a gasp.

"Yes! Tell me. Here is your water." Tiger poured a little down the man's throat. He gagged and spat, begged for more.

"Please…thank you."

She wished she could help him. Felt anger at Gralen. Pushed it down.

"A gang…tell me."

"Jackser thought."

"What?"

"He thought…was Deadheads…"

"Deadheads?"

She feels the press from Gralen. Lets the thought in.

*Deadheads is them that has your brother. Same as Gravelings. But calling themselves Sons of Arroway.*

She would remember that but ignored Gralen for now.

"Where? Where did they travel?"

"…a few sunsteps back – crossed the trail…"

"Can you explain it to us?"

*Gralen can be tracken Deadheads. This one dead.*

"East? Did they move east?"

"Yeah. Can you help me? I feel funny…can you break this off…are you a healer?"

"No. I think if we take this out, you will die faster."

The man groaned, nodded.

"I thought…you look so different, maybe you're special. You can save us." The man was delirious now. "We are starving everywhere. I have a child, Reta. She will die. She has no mother."

Tiger tried to push that information away, but it had already gotten inside and now she would have to carry it. The man's already pale face lost all color.

"Listen…the Deadheads. Tell me –"

"…trying to make…weapon…power source. Deep under. They have electric light."

"Impossible!" Nahim stepped forward, brought

88

his face close to the dying man's,

"It is. True. Nephilim."

"The sweepers have cleaned this land, there is nothing left." Nahim's eyes were glittering moons.

"…so thirsty."

But when Tiger finally brought the waterskin again to the man's lips he was dead.

# Chapter 9

*When the stars threw down their spears,*
*And watered heaven with their tears,*
*Did he smile his work to see?*
*Did he who made the Lamb make thee?*
-William Blake

The blade from the sky was pressed to the thread, ready to tear through. The Deadheads must not take her brother underground. She sliced into her arm almost without thinking, drew more blood than was wise. The biting flies and parasites swarmed her after that. Gralen was certain that if the Deadheads hadn't already reached their lair, they would by late the next morning. If it came to it, Tiger would go inside after her brother, even in the face of certain death. But how to find the doorway? All around them, the road was increasingly lined with the cavernous yawning faces of collapsed habitations, many of them as large as ten Tar Garden huts.

They were travelling east. The sun was setting. They did not speak. On the bodies of the dead men, they found nothing but bone-knives and some dried berries. Gralen moved quickly, anxious to pick up the trail of the Deadheads. Aside from the crunch of branches under his large feet, Nahim trailed quietly behind Tiger, seemingly deep in thought. He had tied his long black hair behind his head with a length of thick green vine.

After some time, the ground became misshapen all around them. More of the unnatural edifices stuck up, stubborn. These vine-covered, moss-hidden structures peered at them with pitch-dark eyes. Animals scurried into them for cover. Some of the structures were enormous, jutting up above the trees. The vines and green of the jungle grew upward with them, twisted around long forgotten stone.

"We come near the heart of one of the former great cities of man." Nahim took a few quick steps and caught up to Tiger, suddenly animated.

Ahead, Gralen was bent to the trail. Something howled in the thicker jungle to the south. The sun was falling quickly in its steps. Soon all dark night would fall.

"Here." Gralen pointed to the ground with a thin, four fingered hand.

"I don't see anything."

Gralen pointed southeast.

"They moven less than four sunsteps ahead. If we moven in night, we maybe finden them before they go under."

Gralen moved ahead. Beckoned. His full energy had emerged as the last rays of the sun began to fall. His eyes began to take on a bright yellow shine. The thought of following those bouncing orbs into the pitch dark unnerved her. She thought of the exploded heads of the men. She thought of the child, Reta, her father pinned dead to a tree. The beasts of the woods would have found him there by now.

Tiger looked south. Wanted to push on. Pushed the urge back inside herself. What would Sai have done? She saw even larger shapes sticking up above the trees in the dying orange light, saw something slink down from the top of one of them. *Come and*

*See*.

"Gralen, we must rest. We are travelling in their land now. Their comfort may have slowed their progress. We can't risk them hearing us approach in the dark."

They set up a rough camp a few paces from the broken road, to the east – where to their surprise – an older, narrower road revealed itself. There was food everywhere, hidden in the darkness, hanging from the trees – but the risk of poison and unseen animals stopped them from eating.

"My father always said that if you try to eat in the jungle, sooner or later, the jungle will eat you." Tiger said.

"The more I hear of him, the more I like your father. What was his name?"

"Avo."

Nahim repeated the name, under his breath.

"Did you eat the meat of animals in the dessert?"

"Whenever we could get them."

"Here the beasts are many. Even us Eloh-Hakim must be cautious, there are some that Those Who Watch have placed here to keep us from straying. But we do not eat meat. To eat the flesh of any creature is against the Law." Nahim grew silent again.

Tiger lay back, against the pile of bigleaf Nahim had collected for them all. Gralen was suddenly nowhere to be seen. It had been many nights since Tiger had slept. Tonight was no exception. The forest sounds nearer. Louder. Darkness absolute.

Her hands slipping.

Couldn't grasp it. Can't grip the thread.

# Chapter 10

*Tyger! Tyger! burning bright*
*In the forests of the night,*
*What immortal hand or eye*
*Dare frame thy fearful symmetry?*
-William Blake

She woke. Knew it was the last day, for good or ill. *Last cut.* Brought the bone-knife down across the other nine, re-opening all the wounds. In the first of the daylight, the trail was visible even to Tiger. It was fresh.

"We are not far behind." The giant said. "I can smell them."

A trail of flattened leaf led away from the road and Gralen had found remnants of a camp. Tiger saw impressions along the base of a tree where people had lay sleeping, perhaps only one or two sunsteps before. For the first time in days, she spooled in the thread, drew it tight. She felt the pressure of the invisible blade more than ever, but Tarren was within reach. Gralen motioned for them to move ahead. There was a form at his feet. Tiger's heart began to thump. She must not think that it could be him. It could not be him.

Not him.

"Aichlan," she said, without emotion.

The man had been kind. She had sat on his knee, less than eight years ago while he told her stories about Saxon Arroway. Hopeful legends about a second coming, about a new world; a paradise, The Watchers driven away. He had been a good man. And now, she was only glad he wasn't

Tarren. They had cut his throat. His skin was not yet fully cold.

"We have to hurry. If they make it underneath, all is lost."

Tiger and Gralen began to run. Nahim strode. The trail twisted down labyrinthine passageways that wove through ruins more overgrown and blasted with each step.

At midday they were forced to stop and rest. Even Nahim was winded. Roots twisted up through the remnants of the human city: strange towering structures of large stone and low-lying piles of brick and rubble. Parts of once great structures remained, leaning strangely, high above their heads, supported by jungle that had grown in as framing; perhaps replacement for metal ripped free centuries ago by the massive sweeper ships that scoured the land. Tiger could hear birds again, singing from the sunlit canopies of the taller structures. Other animals moved in the hollow of the ancient buildings. Eyes gleamed. Slanted rays of light peaked through in places and pooled on the ground; the snaken collected in writhing balls, drinking up the hot sun.

"Tiger." Nahim whispered, from where he sat a small distance away.

The fact that he did not speak in his usual booming voice alarmed her. She looked at him. He was pointing ahead on the trail. Tiger saw nothing. Looked around. Looked again.

"Where is Gralen?" She said quietly. He seemed to have vanished again. Nahim just shook his head and pointed again to the trail in front of them.

"Look. Beyond the snaken."

95

She followed the direction of his pointed finger. Still saw nothing. Then...*a foot*. And the foot was attached to a leg. The leg vanished under a large frond. She kept staring. The foot moved. Just a little. And then she saw something else. Further ahead, in the middle of the sunken path between the buildings, the leaves of the low bushes were rustling. She saw backs – bent to conceal – creeping away through the green. They had stumbled into the midst of the Deadheads they were tracking.

Tiger got up, looked over at Nahim. She pulled out her bone-knife and applied snaken poison to its blade. Nahim got carefully to his feet, squeezing his large hands into fists and looked over at her. Then, Gralen spoke in her head.

*They here. We close to their underground place. Seens us. Heard Nahim. Trying to escape under. Must stop them! Kill!*

Tiger crept forward. Nahim moved even more carefully. A loud cry. All around them, bushes shook to life. From inside the shattered holes of the fallen city, Deadheads leapt out at them with weapons. Some gleamed in the light. Metal. Ahead, Tiger saw several of them spring up. There – ahead. The captives, grown weak, had slowed the raiders down. They were being carried.

Then, she saw him. Her brother Tarren was unconscious, his body dangling limp over the shoulder of one of the men. Then they disappeared around a bend in the trail.

"Tarren!"

She rushed forward, even as she was attacked from the side. Saw the glint of a blade towards her ribs; saw the pale flesh of the bare skull of a

Deadhead. She turned, too late to stop the coming blow. But a rock the size of her fist collided suddenly with the pale skull and the deep lined eyes that had locked onto her were obliterated in a spray of blood, bone and brain. The jagged blade sliced into her coat and only severed the strap of her waterskin. She looked back.

"Sai!" She yelled, as the old man, half-running and half-limping, staggered towards her.

"Tiger-Ghan, watch out!"

Another Deadhead rushed her, knife and sharp teeth flashing. Nahim's massive hands lashed out and plucked the man from the ground. Nahim tossed the Deadhead hard by the ankles into one of the sunken hovels. Tiger could hear the man's bones shatter under his skin as he collided with the old stone. Blood erupted from his mouth and eyes. He twitched only a moment.

"Don't let them get under!" Nahim called, running along the path. Some of braver Deadheads stayed in a cluster to challenge him and were crushed in a mass of writhing pulp. One of their weapons found its mark in Nahim's side, but the giant moved on as though nothing had happened, the weapon waving wildly with each step.

"Come on!" She yelled to Sai. The old man's eyes were fixed, fascinated on the form of the giant.

"Sai. He's helping us. Hurry!" They pressed forward. Absurdly, she began to recite the words of her poem in her head. *Tyger Tyger burning bright.* Three more Deadheads appeared, no match for Tiger in her rage and Sai in his experience. *In the forests of the night.* Her bone-knife found its home quickly between the ribs of one and then in the soft shallow between the neck and chin of another. *What immortal hand or eye.* Sai broke the arm of the third Deadhead and forced the man's own jagged knife up into his own heart. Tiger felt her father's magic at play with that of the poem. Would it be enough?

More blood. Yells of pain came from ahead as Nahim brought two Deadheads together. He dropped them, tangled as though they shared one mind. *Could frame thy fearful symmetry?* Still Gralen was nowhere to be seen. *In what distant deeps or skies burnt the fire of thine eyes?*

"Come any closer and this boy dies."

It was a brutishly large, older Deadhead with twisted scars on his upper right forehead. Tiger could see the hole in his skull where the skin dipped in, kissing the brain. *In what furnace...* the words of the poem stopped running through her mind then. Here was the Deadhead Ghan. She felt certain he was the one that had killed her father. He held Tarren under the arms and had a toothed blade against the flesh of her brother's throat. There were two other Deadheads, one at each side of him, nervously eyeing both Nahim and something else off to the other side. The giant stood motionless beside Tiger in the middle of the cracked dirt and vine-covered road. Nahim's own eyes were not fixed on the Deadheads. His gaze was locked to Tiger's left, on Gralen. She looked over. Gralen stood in the shadow of a fallen building, his bow raised and a pointed arrow knocked and ready, aimed directly at the gnarled old Deadhead. He'd been holding them there. She allowed herself finally to feel trust in him. Sai and Tiger stopped next to Nahim.

"Let him go." She said.

"The boy stays with us. He is everything."

"Give him to me and you may yet live." Gralen hissed and pulled the bow tighter.

"I know this creature. It will not let us live. Nor you, if you suffer it any longer. Get it to lower the weapon."

"No."

Nothing happened. None of them moved. There was only a shifting of eyes.

Tiger could see where they had been meaning to escape to when Gralen had stopped them. There was a round hole in the ground, with a misshapen rock lid that had been slid aside. As she waited, she held her bone-knife, point down to the ground. A single drop of the venom fell and stained a small rock.

The large Ghan sneered at them all. Then looked at Gralen.

"If we cannot have the child, nor can you." He began to draw the knife toward Tarren's throat. Tiger felt the thread pressed under the same knife. It was in her very heart. She started forward.

Then, a command.

"Stop!"

Sai, in a voice Tiger barely recognized. The bulky Deadhead looked up. Sai moved forward, out of the shadow and into a splash of sunlight. All eyes shifted to the old man with the pink-fissured scar across his chest and stomach.

"Dark lay the night that long hid the light." Sai said then.

At the words, the Deadhead Ghan's arm faltered. The knife fell slightly.

"And long is the fight to return to the light. My God. Then the rumours were true. You live."

"Give me this boy. He is my warrant."

The man looked to his companions. They were whispering to each other, and seemed to have entirely lowered their guard. Tiger thought she heard one of them say:

"The Mark! The Mark!".

Nahim and Gralen exchanged a look, but neither of them took their eyes from the threat long enough to regard Sai closely.

"I don't understand...my lord, the Eloh-Hakim? The hybrid..."

"They are under my power now." Sai said.

Tiger didn't know what Sai was doing. She prepared to lunge forward with her knife. The snaken poison would paralyze instantly, kill in moments. But incredibly, the knife of the large man dipped further away from her brother's throat.

"Set the boy down. He doesn't look well. If he isn't breathing, I will eat your hearts tonight for my dinner."

"My lord, he lives, he lives! See?" The man lowered Tarren to the ground. They could see that he was breathing, shallowly. "But he is hungry. We are all hungry. Starving for meat. We had to eat one of them, on the road. I am sorry my lord. Forgive us. The jungle is spoiled by poison."

"That ends now that I have returned." Sai stepped further forward.

The two younger Deadheads were speaking quickly to each other now in a low tongue that Tiger couldn't make sense of. Suddenly they dropped to the ground, heads against the backs of their hands.

100

The older man looked at them, then at Nahim and Gralen, and finally, he dropped his knife and also fell to the ground.

Sai walked toward the men. Motioned the giant to follow. Nahim did. Gralen hadn't moved. The bow was still raised but it was Sai his eye now focused on.

"Saxon Arroway cannot be killed." Sai said as he neared the three men. "I am eternal renewal. I have risen again. The cycle continues." Tiger heard a sharp intake of breath from Gralen.

Sai looked to Nahim and motioned at the two younger ones. Nahim nodded. *Clever of Sai to invent such a lie to fool these brainless men.* She felt a surge of love for his bravery and loyalty. *Foolish old man that he is.*

"Great leader, we have lived in grave error without you and done harm to many. Below you will find a disgrace to your former empire. Lead our people once more, as you led my grandfather. End this pain we have lived in."

"Gladly." Sai said.

Quickly, from behind the waist of his tattered cloth, he revealed his own faded bone-knife. Bone found bone and blood whipped out across the root and rock as Sai struck a smooth arc across the Deadhead Ghan's throat. The man sighed and fell forward. His surprised face came to rest alongside the callused pads of Sai's feet. Sai nodded to Nahim, and the giant reached down. Two voices and lives were easily crushed in Nahim's grip. The men both writhed briefly in the dirt, clutching their throats, then went still.

A silence followed. In it, Tiger could hear

everything. The echo of Deadheads shouting, deep in the tunnels below. The thick breath of Nahim and the thin, ragged whistle in the chest of her weakened brother. She heard the blood still leaking with a weak splash onto the rock. She heard Gralen's calculating thoughts scurrying just out of reach. Heard her own heart bounding. She also imagined she heard one magic thing as she knelt and cradled Tarren's head against her: the re-spooling of an invisible thread. Standing bent yet somehow far taller than she remembered, in the midst of them all, stood an old man. She could hear nothing from him.

"Never fair." Said Gralen. "Was never right. They should take Gralen."

He swung the bow and pointed it at Sai. "Giving me the Starchild, Arroway. This arrow poisoned."

"Check-nay Mo-Kesh, Gralen." Said Sai and moved slightly, so he was positioned in front of where Tiger sat with Tarren. "No."

"Foolish. I will destroy your brain with a thought."

"You can try. I have had many years to learn to close my mind to your kind."

"Sai?" Tiger saw tears splashing down on Tarren's face before she realized she was crying.

The old man turned to her.

"Do not worry child, he cannot hurt you. He does not know."

"What doesn't I know?" Gralen said.

That's when Nahim laughed. His deep rolling booms surprised them all.

"Why, which is the Starchild, of course! Silly

creature. Even the Starchild doesn't know. Your powers won't work on me Gralen. Any harm to Arroway and I shall squeeze everything vital out of you."

"And violate the code?" Gralen hissed. "Thinken not."

Gralen met Sai's gaze. Sai buckled and seized his head, yelled out. Nahim started forward just as Gralen loosed the arrow. It was a powerful bow.

The arrow found its mark deep in Nahim's abdomen.

Vaguely, Tiger was aware that Tarren had come to and was trying to say something to her. The light played on his weakened face and his lips formed familiar shapes. But she couldn't hear what it was.

All sound had been sucked away for this moment. Without thinking, she had connected with Gralen's mind, but it was dark and slippery. It tried to get away, to fold in on itself. She held it, just like one would hold a ripe piece of fruit. She tightened her grip. Waited. His eyes met hers.

She squeezed.

# THE END